PENGUIN BOOKS

MARINE LIFE

Linda Svendsen received an M.F.A. from Colum-
bia University. Her stories have appeared in *The
Atlantic*, *Saturday Night*, *StoryQuarterly*, and
other magazines, and have been anthologized in
The O. Henry Prize Stories and *Best Canadian
Stories*. She also writes for television and film.
She currently lives in Vancouver, where she
teaches creative writing at the University of
British Columbia.

MARINE

LIFE

.

LINDA

SVENDSEN

PENGUIN BOOKS

PENGUIN BOOKS

Published by the Penguin Group

Penguin Books USA Inc., 375 Hudson Street, New York, New York 10014, U.S.A.

Penguin Books Ltd, 27 Wrights Lane, London W8 5TZ, England

Penguin Books Australia Ltd, Ringwood, Victoria, Australia

Penguin Books Canada Ltd, 10 Alcorn Avenue, Toronto, Ontario,
Canada M4V 3B2

Penguin Books (N.Z.) Ltd, 182–190 Wairau Road, Auckland 10, New Zealand

Penguin Books Ltd, Registered Offices:
Harmondsworth, Middlesex, England

First published in the United States of America by
Farrar, Straus & Giroux 1992
Published in Penguin Books 1993

1 3 5 7 9 10 8 6 4 2

AUTHOR'S NOTE

I am grateful to the following publications, in which some of these stories appeared in
earlier form: *The Atlantic*: "Who He Slept By" and "Heartbeat"; *Western Humanities Review*: "Flight"; *Northwest Review*: "Boxing Day"; *Epoch*: "Klingons"; *Agni Review*: "The
Edger Man"; *Prairie Schooner*: "Marine Life"; *Saturday Night*: "White Shoulders."
"Who He Slept By" and "Flight" were also printed in *Best Canadian Stories* (1981 and
1987); "Heartbeat" appeared in *Prize Stories 1983: The O. Henry Awards*.

ACKNOWLEDGMENTS

I would like to thank the National Endowment for the Arts, the Canada Council, the New
York Foundation for the Arts, British Columbia Cultural Services, the Mary Ingraham
Bunting Institute at Radcliffe College, the Wallace Stegner Fellowship at Stanford University, the MacDowell Colony, and the Banff Centre of the Arts for their support. I am
also indebted to my family, Lucy Smith, and, in particular, Nancy Packer.

THE LIBRARY OF CONGRESS HAS ASSIGNED THE FOLLOWING
CATALOG CARD NUMBER TO THE HARDCOVER:
LC 92–71539
(cip data available)
ISBN 0-374-10088-8 (hc.)
ISBN 0 14 02.3048 3 (pbk.)

Printed in the United States of America
Set in Bodoni

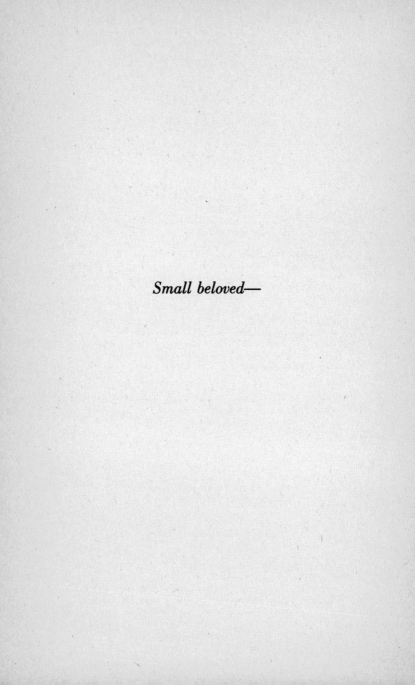

Small beloved—

God setteth the solitary in families.

PSALM 68

MARINE LIFE

WHO HE SLEPT BY

First our mother, June, although I can't swear. Some summer afternoon, hot in Montreal, after a cool wipe and a quick caress of talcum, she might have lain down beside him on a blanket in shade, or in the darkest room in the house, venetian blinds tight. Anyplace that would ease the chafing. Ray's eyes would close and she'd talk to her baby. *Who's a muggy boy? Who's my sticky? Who's a little heat wave?* She wouldn't nap; with her tongue, she might worry an ice cube into a suggestion of snow, and study Ray and wonder if he'd contract rashes she'd never heard of or seen. She was always on the lookout for treachery, crawling or flying or freakish.

The coolest spot may have been under the grand piano. After settling Ray, she would practice her winter repertoire. Softly, "Jingle Bells," "Frosty." (When I was a child she did this, too, exerting a maternal power over weather. *Listen, I'll put a bite in the air.* And after her concert, the room seemed somehow lighter, chillier.) Ray might have glimpsed her foot nodding on the pedal. Maybe this was when he acquired a predisposition for ladies' feet and ankles, and later, when he could view the keyboard, for fingers and flexible wrists. "Watch her tickle those ivories," he'd say when he was older.

Ray's father prospected for asbestos. When he was away, staking claims, Mum probably carried Ray into their wide double bed. She watched him breathe; she said she could watch her babies—each one of us, Ray, Irene, Joyce, and me—breathe for hours. Anticipating their eventual arch, she traced his eyebrows with a finger dampened by saliva. *Even if I was blind,* she'd say, *I could pick my baby out of an orphanage.* She could honestly assert this, not only because she knew Ray's shape and weight, but because the scent of her own mouth was upon him, implicit.

They would sleep facing each other, a human palm apart. If dreams leave the body in breaths, as evil spirits enter after sneezes, who knows what his gentle inhalation drew.

I don't know; in 1940 I was not alive. When there are no early memories, I invent them or go without. In Ray's case, my brother's, I do a little of both. When I was six, he was twenty. I turned twenty, he was thirty-four. He had always been old enough to invent me.

Our mother believed what little she read. When she

first moved to Quebec, before Ray's birth, she noticed that all the bridges were named Pont. On the west coast a different name existed for every crossing—Lion's Gate, Capilano, Patullo. She thought it must be so disorienting for the French with this Pont Bridge, Pont Bridge everywhere.

Then, at a particularly somber birthday supper, Ray's, some years ago, our mother mentioned the report of an American doctor. She urged this newspaper filler into the realm of premonition and hindsight through her tone of voice. She altered its impact, the same way she had influenced seasons, raised and lowered temperatures, when we were children. "He says who you sleep by determines your dreams. That's something to consider." Then Robert, our stepfather, presented the lit cake and Mum asked Ray to make a wish.

In 1959, Ray was nineteen, two fathers wiser, and working as a spare at Vancouver Wharves. His first girlfriend, Velma, worked in a beauty parlour doing manicures and shampoos. One Sunday they drove to Spanish Banks and Mum sent me along. She must have read that sibling responsibility curbed passion.

As soon as their towels kissed sand, they sent me on errands. After delivering their fish and chips, I made a separate trip for each condiment. Salt, ketchup, vinegar. They sent me for 7-Up, straws, ice cream, and extra napkins, for the transistor radio baking on the dashboard.

"Go look for shells," Ray said when I came back from the parking lot. "Go dig a hole to China."

Velma was usually very friendly. Skinny and quiet, she brought spoils from the salon: Adorn, nail hardeners, hairnets that would strangle goldfish. She let me hold the heated towel while she shampooed Ray's hair; this usually took half an hour. She moved her hands every imaginable way, massaging with fingertips and knuckles, tapping, tugging, scratching his head as if seeking entrance. And then rinses. Egg yolk, flat beer, lemon rinse for highlight, baking soda for manageability, and vinegar for purity. She wrapped the towel around his head and they shuffled to his bedroom to use our mother's hairdryer. Velma would leave me with a new shade of polish and instructions. Always stroke away from yourself, she told me.

At the beach that day, I squirmed closer to her oiled body. When I grew up I wanted to dye my hair her colour.

"Go pick up litter," Ray suggested. "Make yourself useful to society."

"Raymond," Velma said.

He handed me a dime. "Treat yourself to the trampolines."

"Where?"

"Across from the concession."

"I don't want to jump."

"I'll make you want to jump."

I bounced with other kids, flags of noisy colour, in the

air. At the peak of each jump, I scanned the beach, trying to distinguish Ray and Velma from the other sunbathers. But they blended with all the other bodies and I stretched out, flat, on the trampoline. Through the straps, I stared at the puddles below and knew that the ocean was quietly escaping. Then the guy yelled my time was up.

Velma was pushing back Ray's cuticles with a coffee stirrer when I returned.

"Back already?"

I didn't answer him.

"Want to be buried in sand, Adele?" He used my name when he meant business.

"No."

Velma suggested we all go in the water, but Ray said I had to remain on shore to frighten beach burglars. I started to cry. Some teenage gals, two towels over, volunteered to guard the site if they could change the station on our radio. Ray said, "Okay. But, Adele, stay in the shallow part."

I stood in water up to my knees, listlessly filling a bright yellow pail with the waves I met, then emptying them out.

They went far beyond my depth. Velma hoisted herself onto Ray's shoulders, her thighs clenched around his neck, and he sang "Blow the Man Down," something nautical. They laughed and splashed, Velma shielding her hair with a free hand, protecting a recent tint. I saw Ray toss Velma into the water and push her shoulders under the surface. Then her head. Everything suddenly seemed silent, as it had when I'd looked below the trampoline, and then Velma emerged, gasping, and started paddling towards me.

"You dink," she called Ray.

Ray floated on his back.

When he joined us on shore, afterwards, Velma looked up at him. "What gets into you?"

He said he was only teasing, couldn't she take a joke, didn't she know he was the Purple People Eater?

They didn't talk. Ray turned his face in the other direction, towards the Pacific Ocean. I packed wet sand into my pail, turned it upside down, and eased out castles. I dug narrow moats around them until I was bored.

I thought Ray was asleep. Velma's hand rested on the small of his back, her nails bright as the buoys bobbing in the distance. Crouching beside him, I avoided his cheek and then carefully lifted the eyelid; I wanted to see his eye drifting and vulnerable. But his eye, unmoving, gazed directly at me. He wasn't really asleep; he was pretending.

A mermaid cupping her blue breast: Ray and our cousin Jackson had identical tattoos on their forearms. They also longshored together.

After rinsing cargo sulphur from their eyes and showering, they spent their evenings fishing for diversion. They parked on mountaintops for optimum shortwave reception and once tuned in Hong Kong. Witnessed demolition derbies and sometimes crossed into Washington State, where bars served until dawn. They met sullen Nootka sisters at hotels near the harbour, loved them rude and slow, and asked for Indian burns. Ray saved brassieres that he and Jackson identified by cologne and sweat rings—"Sue in October. 38C." He stashed the collection in his glove compartment.

The winter of 1964, Ray and Jackson sat home with girlfriends and Cheezies to watch hockey. After the playoffs, Jackson became engaged to Pat and decided to enlist with the RCMP. "Jackson's going to be a Dudley," Ray commented. "A Do-Right."

At Jackson's wedding, that June, Ray acted as usher. He was supposed to be the best man, but Jackson's brother had pulled the longer straw.

Ray started drinking before the ceremony, lacing his breakfast juice with white rum. After our mother and Robert departed, he offered me a taste. "You're old enough to be corrupted."

"I like it," I said.

"Drink up."

On our way to pick up Ray's date, Nadine, I honked the horn indiscriminately and Ray made a few U-turns. He turned the tightest U's. We had devoted the previous afternoon to folding Kleenex into frail blossoms and attaching them to the car as if they grew there naturally. I climbed over the seat when Ray opened the front door for Nadine. Do something about those rolling bottles, he told me, and I placed my white patent-leather shoes on them. Nadine never complimented the car; she spoke in serious tones about her Arabian's fetlock.

Nadine lived in Shaughnessy, the rich section of Vancouver, and worked for a travel agency, Funseekers. Twice a year, she holidayed in Waikiki. Twice a week, she performed her equestrienne routines. Ray attended her events at the Agrodome and would sometimes allow me to come. Children under twelve were admitted free.

I liked listening to Ray watch her. He predicted her moves, her strategies with doting accuracy. *Watch her bite flank with that spur. Now she's neck-reining. She knows how to place her weight.* The horse responded to the slightest suggestion of her thigh; Ray was correct. Even her tongue moistening her lips seemed to indicate a specific command—I could sense that. She wore boots and her nails were as blunt as her conversation, and she kept them that way intentionally; if they were longer, they hampered grooming. She always seemed to be looking ahead to the next obstacle, past it.

When the judging was concluded, Ray met her at the stables. Once, he had pushed a finger, sideways, across her mouth. "Chafing for a bit?" he'd asked.

She had slapped his hand. "Smarten up." Then smiled, apologetically.

She smiled often at the reception; she congratulated Jackson and Pat. In the receiving line, Ray usurped the position of best man and stood beside Jackson, embracing every woman. "Ray the Ush," he introduced himself. Nadine politely joined my parents and me. I asked her opinion about a television series starring a talking horse; she said she'd never heard of it. Smiling vaguely, she stared at Ray.

Ray waited until the second chorus of "Telstar" before cutting in on Jackson and Pat's first dance as newlyweds. He spun the laughing Jackson across the floor and then they returned to Pat, giggling and pale, enfolding her in their arms. The three clung to each other in the spotlight.

Later I saw Ray and Nadine attempting the beer-barrel polka; she led. I wanted to twist with my brother, who had taught me, but he declined. "Got to save my strength for the garter," Ray said. "Go ask an uncle."

When Jackson tossed the garter and Pat her bouquet, neither Ray nor Nadine was present. I hoped: elopement, riding lessons under Nadine's expert guidance, saddle sores I would never mention. At the gift table, Irene, Joyce, and I were appraising three toasters, deciding which ones we'd return, when Mum accosted us.

"Where's your brother?"

We searched the cabaret; our parents knew he was not in exemplary driving condition. Exhausted, they chose to assume that Nadine had commandeered the wheel and the couple were safely at home, sipping coffee and comparing test patterns. Nothing else.

Ray's car was not parked in the street.

I couldn't sleep; I knew where they were. At the stables, measuring each other's height in hands, or snuggling in straw and being nuzzled by long-nosed horses with white stars or blazes. Except for his socks, they probably had taken off all their clothes, hung them on nails, and kissed. I fell asleep picturing a soft foal watching them, whinnying, and forgot to slide the wedding cake under my pillow.

Jackson called in the morning. He told us Ray had spent the night with him and Pat, at their apartment, and had just left. He said they'd fried eggs and talked until five, about women, the waterfront, unions, and then passed out on the living-room rug, side by side.

Fourteen years later, Jackson stood as godfather to my son. He wore the distinctive red jacket of the Mounted Police. We reminisced about our weddings and he mentioned Ray's impromptu visit, how understanding Pat had been. Jackson laughed. "Ray just wanted to talk. He wanted to talk about how hard it was to be a man." Then he looked at me, sober, as if for corroboration.

Ray spent two weeks in California and peripheral Mexico, a town called Dos Reales, late in 1966. Although he had just earned his forklift operator certificate, he was restless and discontented at the piers. His friends convinced him to travel and so he worked weekends, night shift, double time, time and a half. He saved.

I still have his postcard of Alcatraz, obscured by fog, with some scribbled message about the Birdman. And I clearly remember his tan, next to our winter skins, making him seem like a guest when he returned.

We were looking at my slides of Europe, many years ago, when he mentioned this trip. Ray and I were thirty-five and twenty-one, old and comfortable enough to talk openly. I'd just admitted that the true story wasn't revealed in the photographs, and told him about making love with a stranger on the Hovercraft between England and France. He listened, then asked if I wanted to hear about south of the border.

Dos Reales: He breakfasted at poolside, tequilas, and decided to walk to the main part of town. He was amazed that donkeys still carried sacks of avocados, amazed that poinsettias still grew wild.

A procession of twenty women, veiled in black, crept by him. Hands stroked rosaries, and their knees must have been scratched raw by the rocky paths and highways. Somebody explained that it was Lent and these women had travelled miles on a pilgrimage of repentance. Ray was amazed that people still practiced devotion.

In town he browsed for souvenirs—a poncho for Mum, a sombrero for our stepfather, Robert. A young boy no older than fourteen, whose voice had just begun to change, asked Ray if he would like to make conversation with his sister. Hesitantly he added, "Ten American dollars. Very pretty tits."

"Mañana," Ray replied, and strolled away. But the boy persisted and soon Ray thought some Mexican pussy might not be a bad idea. The market was crowded and hot; it had been a while.

Ray understood they would go to a hotel or the back of some cantina. Instead, the boy took him to a squat adobe house, near the beach, and introduced him to Capulina.

"*Gracias*, Mr. Ray," she said.

She was only twelve, with hair falling below her waist, hiding tiny moles on her back. She invited him into her bedroom and he noted the sagging cot, the crucifix over the door, a pastel of the Virgin on Capulina's trunk. She got on her knees.

He told me he stayed with her all that afternoon, woke and ate a late supper with her aunt and brother, then spent the entire evening. She wanted to learn English, he said. So he counted numbers on her slender fingers and he taught her nouns—earlobe, hard, cut-offs, bruise.

He marvelled at the tininess and tirelessness of her hands and mouth. He watched her bathe his feet and slip her tongue around the toes and soles. During the night she slept on top of him, a full smaller shadow.

For months after that, he had worried he might have caught something incurable: a desire for skilled little girls.

I shut off the projector and we sat in the dark.

"It was great," he said, then reminded me: "You were twelve years old then, too, Adele."

Ray married Merry, who did not deliver the promise of her name. Merry of the backcombed hair, who teased herself into an optical illusion six inches taller and wore

slippers so fuzzy her feet looked shocked. She worked at
the stationery store and her envelopes arrived as fre-
quently as advertising flyers. While Ray seduced her,
she courted Mum, my sisters, and me. *Greetings from
Merry, forever. From Merry's mansion to yours.* Cards
with sickly elves and pictures of wheat bending in the
wind. She made me skeptical of good intentions.

Merry bore this thoughtfulness and legibility into the
bedroom. I knew Ray had slept with her, because her
name would be written on him somewhere. Where the
watchband had been, Merry, or on the jugular, Merry,
and once, when his boot happened to be off, on the big
toe, Merry.

He loved her; it was obvious. He spent evenings folding sheets with her at the laundromat, making corners
meet. He visited a butcher with her and bragged about
pricing cuts, the economics of freezing. When she strug-
gled with situps, he secured her feet and watched her
unfailing chin rise towards him. He paid for her fillings,
stopped seeing other women, and worked steadily, after
a drinking suspension of three months. The kitchen table in his apartment was strewn with Merry snaps, and
there were a select few by his bed, signed.

Ray slept with Merry for three years, 1968–1971,
more in sickness than in health. Early in their marriage,
he must have made the mistake of tactless or embel-
lished confession. Perhaps, after a brisk shower together
and a slower drying out, when talk comes easily, she
had inquired about the aquatic woman nestled in his

arm. The past. And Ray, confident in her sympathy, had told her about Velma, little Capulina, the skittish horse-back rider. About Joanne at Hertz; Dallyce, whom Merry had focused upon in our parents' movies of a New Year's Eve.

Consequently, Merry convinced herself of his infidelity. An excursion for cigarettes suggested a cheap trick. Lilacs, and he was wooing a florist. The waterfront raised possibilities: stowaways, overtime, empty warehouses. At noon, she delivered his lunch, sandwiches and a cold beer, to the docks, sniffed his clothes, and kissed him.

To pacify her, Ray stayed home and watched television; she became jealous of soap women and accused him of fantasizing. Once, she thought she caught him jerking off to a provocative commercial.

Ray worked graveyard shift. He hoped her sleep might be a respite for them both. In the morning he found her crumpled on the couch, curled and defenceless. She was still dressed in her clothes of the day before and had covered herself with an old car coat. In her grogginess, she asked him, "What am I going to do?"

Ray held her close. "You have to trust," he said.

He drank more often; she paged him at bars and tailed him in her car. "You must not love me, because you drink," she said.

He said, "I drink because I love you."

One night he hit her, knocked her across the kitchen and against the stove. She called the police and Ray was arrested for assault. Dishevelled and quiet, she bailed him out the next morning and dropped charges. Ray guessed she suspected the policewomen.

During the next year, Merry developed a series of terminal illnesses that demanded Ray's time and sobriety. He chauffeured her to X-rays, ECGs, blood tests, checkups. There was talk of brain tumours, cancer. The doctors were indefinite; she gave herself six months every three months, until her pregnancy.

I visited Ray and Merry for a weekend and helped them prepare the baby's room. We painted the walls an undersea hue, a muted aquamarine, and sanded the floors. Diapers, rubber pants, a white basket holding ointments and pins—Ray showed me these as if they were rare discoveries. Merry showed us how she would pant during labour.

She miscarried. I don't like to think how or why. Ray didn't sleep in their bedroom when she was in the hospital; he stayed in what would have been the child's room, wrapped in a sleeping bag.

When she was released, Merry didn't call Ray as they had arranged. She took a taxi home instead, dropped off her suitcase, and gathered some things, then proceeded to Ballantyne pier.

It was a drizzling Vancouver day and Ray was driving a tractor in the huge hold of a ship, the *Argo*. He levelled hills of salt, pushing them into the loading apparatus. Merry ignored the trespassing and danger signs, the foreman, and walked up the gangway, then along the deck to Ray's hold. She screamed to him, sixty feet below, and when he didn't hear, because of the noise of the motor and conveyor belts, she unpacked her bag and pitched the layette into his line of vision. She threw diapers, bibs, a terry giraffe, a rattle.

He quickly shut off the engine and asked her what in hell she was doing.

And she wept, because he wanted her pregnant so he could fuck other women, because her baby had gone to Limbo.

Ray met Sophia at a hotel near the grain elevators. She was a barmaid. She gave him free rum, soon followed by room and board. I saw them together only once, at the dinner our parents gave for Ray's birthday. I was majoring in anthropology and pondered Ray and his amour with the biases of a sophomore. I studied them as I would have a culture on the verge of extinction.

Ray lounged in discount chic: a shiny polyester shirt with sunsets sinking on the pockets. Sophia wore some sort of a baseball cap and a neck brace, because of an old car injury. She was blond and Portuguese and her voice was husky from two decades of cigarettes. They both spoke the same language. "Adele, hang loose," Ray said. "Yeah, no be so uptight," Sophia said.

Ray had been laid off from work and Mum asked about his unemployment insurance. He hadn't applied for it. He blamed his laziness on a dose of mononucleosis that had lasted thirty-two years. Sooner or later, he expected compensation. "I live on her tips until then," he said. "I live on her cupcakes," he said to me conspiratorially. It slowly hit me that my brother might be an asshole.

Sophia spoke to me in the basement, where I was killing time stacking coasters. She put her hand on my arm: her nails were chewed halfway to the moons, and skin that should have been exposed to the air was painted with clear gloss.

"You're a smart girl, your brother tells me. He's very proud of you. Do you care for your brother very much?"

I nodded, and she kept on running her sentences together.

She told me she loved Ray very much and that soon they might put a down payment on a camper van, but she was concerned about him. Sophia said she'd been taking Somas for her neck spasm since the accident and the pills were disappearing. She hoped Ray wasn't stealing them. He was so tired lately. He couldn't even get it up anymore, said his penis was crooked since birth.

"I don't want to hear this," I said.

She laughed. "Oh, you're so young. Soon you'll be seeing men."

"I already am." My tone was too defensive.

"Good for you, Adele." She looked sad, as if I'd snubbed her. "Have fun," she said, and walked back upstairs.

Unashamedly, I added Ray to a list: read books outside your field, defrost fridge, call your brother. Sometimes I invited him for lunch and heated up frozen pizza.

I was up late studying for finals when Ray phoned from Sophia's apartment. "Adele," he said, "I can't wake her up."

In the late seventies, I lived in Osoyoos, a village in the Interior, while expecting my second child. Up north, my American husband worked on the DEW, or Distant Early Warning, Line for two months at a time. Bill tracked the sky for the unexpected: a missile, satellites precarious in their orbits, space debris.

Ray visited occasionally; it was only a day's drive from Vancouver. Whenever he disagreed with Gretel, about every six weeks, he arrived with three cases of beer and said, "Know any smart teachers? Any practical nurses?" By Sunday afternoon, he would be anxious to reconcile with his so-called kumquat. I had never met Gretel; she supposedly was a champion swimmer, butterfly stroke, and Ray threatened to bring her Commonwealth medals to prove it. She worked in a delicatessen and kept their larder stocked with sausage and cheeses. He never mentioned Sophia.

One night at dinner, Ray and I discussed the waterfront, how boring he found his job there and how little it meant to him. I tried to make him part of an international scheme, show him his place in the promise of Canada, how he implemented growth: the potash and sulphur from the prairies fertilized Japanese fields, wood chips from our forests provided paper for China, coal heated the steel mills in South America, and grains fed herds on the drifting continents. I worried about being condescending and didn't even convince myself.

He changed the subject. "You have it good," he began. "A house, credit, the kid."

He loved Graham. The last time Ray had stayed, a few weeks back, he had mentioned taking Graham, who was two, and me back with him to view an air show. He launched into the subject again, describing all the loops and spins. Riding on the wing. Skydiving.

"Adele, you've got to see the Blue Angels."

"I know."

"And the Snowbirds, too. They're Canadian."

He mentioned that admission was ten bucks per car, so the more bods the better. Gretel would make sandwiches at the deli and steal them.

I had to find an excuse, because I couldn't tell him I was too frightened to drive with him. He drove recklessly; Graham was two; I was expecting. But I thought, seeing his hurt face, *How can I let him down?*

We stayed up late and watched pornographic films on the French CBC. Staying up late with Ray; it was something I had begged to do as a child. I had faked nightmares and coughs, bit my own arm, anything. Now his companionship was a given.

"I'm beat," I said, before the credits. "Sweet dreams."

"Nighty-nightski," he said.

I covered up Graham and heard Ray pulling out the Hide-A-Bed.

I slept by my brother once. When I was thirteen and he was twenty-seven, we drove to Medicine Hat to visit Jackson and his wife. Our mother insisted I accompany him; I could read maps and watch for careless deer. Plying Ray with the companionship of a little sister, she protected him from dangers: night driving, night drinking.

The first hundred miles we sang old jingles together, about Brylcreem's "little dab" and the Polaroid Swinger: "It's not like a camera, it's almost alive." Ray took a picture of me by a model of the Ogopogo, a monster in Okanagan Lake. After that, when mountains stood in the way of radio, I read, and read by glaciers, Rocky Mountain goats, and foothills; I missed all the natural phenomena. We spoke at gas stations and burger stands. In Calgary, while searching for access back onto the Trans-Canada, Ray said his father, now an oil man, might live there somewhere. To make conversation, I asked if Ray had ever liked my dad, Humphrey, and he said, "Not one iota."

At chapter breaks, I counted how many pages to the end. At the end of a book, I estimated the distances between stops.

On the return trip, we were caught in a prairie storm. Hailstones the size of watch faces pelted the car and Ray couldn't see more than a few feet beyond the headlights. We checked into a small hotel room in a town where the power had failed—two separate rooms. We requested a double with single beds, but that wasn't available.

I didn't undress. I looked out the window at the new lightning—sheet lightning, I found out later—and wondered if I was grounded. People who were struck by lightning often disappeared I knew.

I knocked on Ray's door.

"I'm scared," I said.

Ray had already been asleep. He was wearing only his undershorts, and his face was creased from the pillow. "Crawl in," he said.

Pulling up the sheet, I laid on top of it and settled the other blankets, those on my side, over me. I wanted to maintain our respectful distances. Ray was too tired to notice this peculiarity. He turned over on his stomach and was soon breathing evenly.

I watched the flashes outside the window, each one a shock, illuminate his ribs, spine, the globe of his head, and I saw the town suddenly light up again in unfamiliar neon. I heard the thunder, moving east, and I slept soundly, safely.

FLIGHT

t was Queen Victoria's birthday; I remember because the schools were closed and I'd felt slightly guilty all day, as if I should have been someplace else. After beating Penny at Ping-Pong, I biked home. At the bottom of the crescent I could make out my mother and second oldest sister on our front porch. I pedalled hard and pretended I was going to crash into them. "No brakes," I shouted. "Save the children and run for your lives."

At the last second I swerved, crushing a clump of daffodils. They hadn't budged. Joyce still wore sunglasses, although there was nothing to shield her eyes against. "Hi, gang," I said. "Why're you sitting out here in the dark?" The lamp on my bike beamed across their laps and they seemed hypnotized by a family of moths going tizzy in the light. It was then I realized something wasn't right. I said, "What happened?"

"Joyce is leaving Eric," Mum said carefully, and I was struck by that word *leaving*. Joyce had not actually *left* yet, although her body was beside ours and not his. "She's going to stay with us until she's on her feet."

"Oh," I said.

"I'll let her tell you. I'm going to bring the mower in before somebody steals it." Mum stepped over the zigzag of half-cropped lawn and tugged the machine out from under the dogwood. She called over the rattle, "Doesn't the grass smell good?" and disappeared into the garage. She was crying.

I put my arm as far around my sister as I could. Joyce was twenty-four then, ten years older than me. She peaked at six feet, on a full breath, and was pretty— with dark hair, a very long neck, and skin white as rice. She stared over the yard. "Eric couldn't hold a job," she finally said. "There was nothing to eat except Quaker Oats."

This confirmed what I'd heard: Eric was a dreamer. Instead of buying bread or socks, he shopped for airplane parts, and the skeleton of a wing had been suspended in each shabby living room since the honeymoon. He had promised me a flight to Djakarta when he had pro- pellors. He didn't pay bills and made long long-distance calls to an aviator pal in Gander Bay. He used Joyce's name to apply for a phone when the old one was dis- connected. I had thought him shrewd and romantic, and Joyce blessed.

"And he hit me," she said, slowly rolling up her

sleeves to show her right arm, her left. Then she turned, raised the glasses, and I saw that side of her face, and neck, all the rich blue marks.

The next day Mum urged me to skip school to help keep my sister company. I was also supposed to alert her if Joyce stayed longer than ten minutes in the bathroom or glanced at her reflection in a sharp blade. I missed an oral report on French verbs and my friend Penny telephoned to see if I was sick or what. "Joyce's marriage failed," I said. "She has to talk to me about it. This is bigger than French."

"*Très* interesting," she said. "That means Eric's free now, eh?" Penny fancied herself a temptress. She patterned herself on Joyce.

Joyce had wound up with Eric when the family was officially between fathers, although Robert was often around. Our mother, June, had worked two jobs and my brother, Ray, longshored; my oldest sister, Irene, had instructed a Belgian immigrant in English (she'd eventually wed him and proceeded to do boring Belgian things—bake sour pastries, fuss with tulips, and nurse a prim baby daughter). I saw my father and movies on Saturdays. Joyce had quit grade eleven and lolled around the airport with Eric. She could identify unseen objects by their purr in a cloudy sky. They'd married when Eric was wait-listed for ground school. She'd been twenty.

Late that afternoon, Mum rushed out to buy last-

minute onions for supper. Joyce was listening to a
Herb Alpert and the Tijuana Brass cut called "The
Lonely Bull." She didn't want to snack or consult the
Ouija board or talk. "You're haunting me, Adele," she
said.

"Why don't we walk the dog? Groucho could use the
exercise."

"I don't need a nanny." Joyce got up and replaced the
needle at the beginning. The trumpets blared.

I convinced her to bask in the sun because exposure
might hasten the healing of her bruises. She borrowed
two of our mother's bandannas (Eric had used her bathing suit as a hazard flag on a U-Haul and lost it on the
freeway) and wrapped them snugly around her breasts
and hips.

It was hot and our Welsh Corgi, who was as old as me,
panted under an evergreen. After a few minutes, Joyce
asked me to bring out the Crisco. She slathered little
pats of shortening on the tops of her legs, and smeared
the inside of her elbows and thighs until she glistened in
the rusty chaise longue, which I'd also set up.

I opened my French textbook and read about Jacque-
line bumping into Paul at the Arc de Triomphe. The
theme of the new verb list was "getting acquainted." I
looked up from the glossary, after I'd found another
translation, and noticed tears running down my sister's
face. "Hey," I said. I went over and patted her slippery
shoulder.

"I will never love another man," she said. "Never."

"You will," I said, wishing our mother were home.

"You have a whole life ahead, Adele."

"Not really," I said. "Not like you."

When our stepfather came home from the docks, she pulled herself together. Mum grilled cheese on raisin toast, Joyce's favorite, and mashed a potato salad. Joyce wasn't biting, and when Mum asked why, Joyce said she hadn't liked that kind of sandwich since she was a teenager. Robert discussed Eric. "Know what I'd like to do, Beauty?"

"No," Mum said. "What?"

"I'd like to go over there and torch the bastard's plane." He looked Joyce's and my way. "Pardon my Greek, but I'd like to cut off his balls with a dull razor." He meant well, but Mum saw Joyce's solemn face and changed the subject. Robert and Mum eventually decided to phone the skip tracer, whom they'd stalled for months, and deliver their son-in-law's current address. They needed to do something.

I had been lonely in the house, and in the world, after Joyce married Eric. She'd babysat me when I was a tyke and played "Mother, May I Cross the Golden River?," commanding ten dinosaur steps backward until I was out in the street in the traffic. She had threatened to phone the Nazis if I didn't brush my teeth. Then, in our baby dolls in the living room, we had pretended to be Peggy

and little Janet of the Lennon Sisters singing on Law-
rence Welk—

> *Up in Lapland little Lapps do it.*
> *Let's do it,*
> *Let's fall in love.*

I had looked up to her.

One night, when Mum and Robert drove to a nursery,
Joyce brought out a tray of ice and gave me a pedicure
so I would learn how to give her one. While she sucked
the cubes, and clipped and buffed, she talked a bit
about Eric. She felt guilty about leaving him; after all,
everybody fights (she cited Princess Margaret and Lord
Tony, and the bickering couple on *Bewitched*). And she
was hurt: he'd told her no other fool would give her his
virile years and she'd die a shrew.

"But if you'd stayed with him, you'd have died of
malnutrition," I said. "Anyway, when I graduate in three
years, we can live together."

"Right." She switched feet. She didn't seem thrilled.

On Sunday, Mum, Joyce, and I brunched at a pan-
cake house. Mum had deliberated about including
Irene, but Irene's zest usually depressed everybody else.
We ordered crumpets, raspberry jam, and tea.

"Thank God there were no kids, Joyce," Mum said.
"At least you're free to look for work."

"Not yet," I said.

"I think a job would do wonders for your self-respect."
Mum cornered Joyce with her gaze. "You'd be paying
your own way, you'd meet people. It's important to circulate during a separation."

Robert had ushered Joyce to the lawyer a few days
before. She had now legally left Eric. She didn't charge
him with assault, saying the blame was fifty-fifty and
he'd been provoked. Nobody asked how.

"I don't want to circulate, Mother," she said. "And
I'm entitled to welfare."

"Not when you're living in Robert's house. Not when
you're not sick."

"Then I'll move," Joyce said.

"I'll go with you," I said.

Mum banged her spoon against a cup and the young
couple in the booth behind us turned attentively. "Listen," she said. "I've contacted somebody about you,
Joyce." Our mother played piano. Her connection for
Joyce was a store manager she knew from the music
business, who handled fashion shows and star searches.
He understood Joyce's beauty and charm recommended
her as a demonstrator. Mum implied a future in model-
ling.

"I refuse to wear an apron and give away cheese,"
Joyce said.

"Look." Mum spoke earnestly and with love. "You
never listened to anything I said while you were growing
up. Maybe you could give my ideas a shot now."

Joyce slowly dunked a crumpet; our mother sensed a little victory. She picked up the bill.

By the start of June, Joyce had opened a savings account in her own name, gained seven pounds, and seemed shorter. Penny and I caught a bus downtown on a Saturday afternoon to watch her demonstrate.

We saw a ring of umbrellas in front of Woodward's window, and we elbowed our way through the men, muttering, "Press." Joyce, in black terry shorts and tank top, idly pedalled a stationary bicycle. She advertised the ultimate elasticity in panty hose. Her legs, the shade of steeped pekoe, clashed with her pale arms. On a break at the back of the store, Joyce rested against a wall of shoeboxes. "The chain catches," she said. "I've snagged every pair."

Penny and I sympathized with her until the manager tapped his wrist and Joyce headed back to the window. We watched her a while longer, then waved goodbye and searched for a cheap palm reading. We couldn't find one in our price range. Near Victory Square, Penny broached the prospect of Eric again and I said he'd been despondent and volunteered for the air force, which was a lie. She asked where he was stationed.

When we reached home, soaked, Joyce was erasing an answer in her TV crossword. She'd been fired at three o'clock.

Mum couldn't bear to see any woman manless. She and Robert equated Joyce's lost marriage to falling off a horse; she must mount again, the sooner the better. And if Joyce wasn't employed, she'd better find a man who could support her. (Actually Joyce was working again; she'd signed up at Manpower and been temporarily hired by a paper mill taking inventory. She counted bundles of foolscap.) Of course, our parents didn't air their misgivings around Joyce, and I didn't repeat what nobody knew I'd gleaned.

I guessed something was afoot when Mum invited Joyce and me to dine at the Grouse Nest, where she was playing all week. The restaurant crowned a nearby mountain. "You should both dress," she said.

Joyce wore a cream boussac suit of Mum's, and I sweated in kilt and Nordic sweater set. Mum spotted us in the lobby and struck two dramatic chords. I wanted to duck; Joyce flanked the maître d'. At our reserved table, a waiter introduced himself. Dietmar was taller than Joyce and his eyes were the washed-out green of pears. Mum tinkled "Kismet."

"Joyce?" he said. "I hope you have an appetite." He trimmed the wick and lit it. He slipped the linen napkins across our knees. He wore a ring on his left pinky.

"He's what the doctor ordered," Mum said, driving us home in her Impala. She extolled Dietmar's manners and mused about what to barbecue when he came for dinner: sockeye or steak. Joyce twisted the radio dial until she heard something familiar. "Paul Anka," she said. "That's Paul Anka."

Dietmar was our mother's choice; Robert's was Rex, an independent tugboat owner out of Portland, who hauled barges of cedar. He popped in one afternoon, when we all coincidentally happened to be in the backyard, to borrow an adjustable winch. Joyce sunned in Mum's bandannas; Mum checked my conjugations in the shadow cast by a willow. *"Croire,"* she said to me. The test was the next day.

Rex also towered. He had blond hair, whiskers, and the grin of an otter. I liked him.

"Hi." Joyce tightened her top bandanna.

"Hello, Rex," said our mother. "Say hello, Adele."

"Hi there," I said, noting his name was only a consonant away from sex.

"Pull up a chair," said Robert. "What you drinking?"

The men griped about Soviet fishing vessels trespassing in North American waters. Groucho started lapping up Rex's beer, which was in a stein by his feet, and Robert cursed. He threatened to donate the dog to science and I gave him a dirty look. Joyce watched the rock garden as if it perceptibly grew.

Mum interrupted. "Rex, do you keep a girl in every port?"

"Hardly." He glanced at Joyce.

"Why not?"

"Mum," I said.

"Don't have time," Rex said.

"Good for you," Robert said. "I run a harem and they're trouble."

"He's teasing," Mum said.

Joyce stood and stretched, and we stopped talking to admire her. Her ribs still stuck out but she was slightly tanned, the bruises faded; she picked up Mum's poncho and shrugged it on. "What's the boat's name, Rex?"

"No name yet. I'm repainting it. That's why I need the extra winch."

"Oh."

"You should see it when I'm done," he said.

"Soon?" Mum said.

Three days later, Joyce and I boarded Rex's bright boat in English Bay. It was the first of July, Dominion Day, and I was chipper about graduating from grade nine. Penny was suffering at a camp with permafrost a foot below, and I looked forward to Joyce and summer holidays.

Rex let Joyce steer and explained, in a low steady voice, about courtesies of the sea. He pitched me a coil of rope and showed me how to tie a simple knot. Then we ate tuna on kaiser rolls, sipped club soda, and puffed menthol cigarettes.

We droned towards our mooring in twilight. Joyce asked Rex about sound travelling more clearly over water, and he cut the inboard. The waves slapped cheeks. He asked what she was listening for.

Joyce straightened her head. "I don't know," she said.

Rex kissed us good night at our door, but kissed my sister last and longer.

"If you married Rex you'd be an American," I said to her after he'd gone.

"I am married," she said.

A twelve-unit motel on Kingsway hired Joyce as a relief maid. She scrounged skinny bars of soap that we tucked in our boots and gossiped about people she met from different parts of the continent. But they were all motorists and therefore duller and more slobbish than people who flew places. Since Joyce was constantly exhausted, Mum hounded me to finish her chores around the house.

The supper for Dietmar fell on a Monday, when the restaurant was closed. Irene and her husband arrived, bearing perishables and the baby. They were leaving the next day to visit a hamlet outside of Liège where all the surviving Belgian in-laws aged. Irene talked to Joyce and me while squeezing extra heads of iceberg into the crisper.

"Let's face it," Irene said. "Eric was a rat. You need somebody more mature, Joyce."

"He wasn't a rat," Joyce said.

"Why do you still stick up for him?" Irene swivelled, and her eyes searched mine. "He beat her, for God's sake."

Joyce focused on the stack of green heads. "Adele, get my cigarettes from upstairs."

"Later."

Joyce pinched me, hard, on the arm. "Now."

"Don't talk while I'm gone." I dashed upstairs ("Thought you quit," Irene was saying) and grabbed the pack off Joyce's pillow. When I got back, Irene had her arm awkwardly folded around Joyce. She had to reach up.

"I love you," she said.

"I love you, too," Joyce said.

"I want to see you happy."

They both looked at me. They had nothing more to say; they didn't seem to be sisters for a moment.

"Here's the baby." Irene appraised me and let go of Joyce.

"I'm the baby." Joyce took her cigarettes. "Adele's the afterthought." It was the family joke.

Irene bent over the remaining vegetables. "You'll take good care of the animals while we're gone, won't you, Adele?"

I nodded. Robert and Dietmar and Peter, Irene's husband, chuckled outside.

"Who's this Dietmar chap?" Irene said.

During the meal, he snickered at Robert's Newfie jokes, buttered Mum up by saying she was better than Liberace, praised the Low Countries, and doted on Joyce. She enjoyed the attention, but flinched when he picked the slivers of bone from her fish. Irene helped with the dishes, conferred with Robert about a lift to the airport, then Peter whisked his family home. Mum and Robert tied Groucho to his doghouse and turned in strategically early. That left Joyce, Dietmar, and me in the living room. His head was behind hers and he was murmuring something about her nape.

"Do you like music, Dietmar?" I hunted for the polka album.

"No."

Mum called from upstairs, "Adele. Lights out."

"There's no school," I yelled.

"There's no nonsense," she said.

"Good night," Dietmar said to me.

"Going?" I said.

Joyce laughed, then stopped herself. "Exit stage left," she said to me.

In bed with a detective story, I read to the first murder, then skimmed the end. My guess was wrong. Then I heard their footsteps, Joyce's door shutting, and I thought about how modern our family's morals had become. I let my light burn.

Joyce showed up in Dietmar's shirt after midnight and seemed disoriented. "I want to come in," she said.

"You're in."

She stood rubbing the bridge of her nose, the lines of cheekbone, as if reassuring herself of a face.

"You want me to get Mum?" I said.

"No." Joyce lowered herself onto the floor, easing her spine against the boxspring. "What is that man's name?"

"What?" I didn't understand what I'd heard.

"What's his name?"

"Last?"

"First."

"Dietmar," I said. "Dietmar something."

"Oh." She pulled the comforter over her hair.

"What?" I said.

"Nothing," she said.

"Sure?"

"Nothing."

I had to check. "What's *your* name?"

"Joyce."

While Dietmar snored alone next door, we lay backwards in the single bed and shared a pillow. She fell asleep. Her closed eyes flickered in dream and I wondered what Joyce saw in that other world. I touched her cold ear with my finger.

I didn't wake up Joyce on time and she was dismissed from the motel. A non-smoking guest had already complained about ashes in the sink and the owner phoned and claimed her lateness was the last straw. This upset Mum because she'd knocked on Joyce's door in the morning and, when there was no answer, trusted Dietmar had driven her to work. She was shocked to find my sister with me, and called a summit conference before she'd even flossed her teeth.

"What are you going to do now, Joyce?" Mum perched on the top stair and twisted a strand of the shag rug.

"I don't know," she said. "I don't feel so hot."

"She needs sleep," I said.

My mother didn't say anything. After breakfast she dropped us at Irene's fussy brick house on the southern slope. Irene was paying me five dollars a week to feed the bird and the Siamese fighting fish, and to perform humdrum tasks. Joyce tagged along; she didn't want to be alone with the questions, or suggestions, of our mother. While I defrosted the fridge, Joyce spilled a pouch of jacks and impatiently flipped them. "Double bounce," she said.

"Bravo." My fingers stuck to the ice cube tray.

"What's the matter, Adele? You got a chip on your shoulder, too?"

I did. Mum blamed me for harbouring Joyce, letting her oversleep and lose her job. And Joyce was unpredictable: she said she loved Eric, yet slept with Dietmar; she forgot Dietmar's name ten minutes after making love; she pinched me hard. But I didn't say any of that. I gave her the ice. "You always get off scotfree, Joyce."

"What do you mean?"

"You never help. I've got to do the fridge, then vacuum, then clean the birdcage, then make your lunch."

"Where's the vacuum, Delly?"

"Hall closet."

She ducked her head going through the archway and I heard the cord unwinding, a flick, and the monotone whine. She bustled in, holding a long and headless hose, the vacuum floating behind.

"Thanks, Joyce."

"I'll charge you later."

"There's an attachment," I said. "It snaps on."

She quickly did the kitchen, saying "Oops" when a

stray jack clanked in the machine. She advanced to the dining room. After lifting the steaming pots, one by one, and placing them in the freezer, I found the proper brush buried at the back of the closet and took it to her.

Joyce was dangling the hose through the small door of the birdcage. Sesame seeds, gravel, and a plume vanished. Irene's pink finch clung by its beak and claws to the cuttlebone, near the top of the cage.

"Joyce," I yelled.

She raised the tube as slightly, and deliberately, as her chin, and the brilliant bird disappeared.

Our parents hustled Joyce to an Egyptian psychiatrist and he recommended a thorough rest. He comforted Mum and Robert. Their intention had been correct; they were right to try to keep Joyce distracted. But she had possibly been too busy. He admitted her to Hollywood Hospital, a ramshackle mansion in New Westminster. In the fifties, disturbed film stars had recuperated there without hoopla; the asylum was discreet, off the beaten American path.

Mum and Robert didn't let on that Joyce was institutionalized; they told our aunts and acquaintances Joyce was camping in the Interior. They wouldn't even let me visit until the end of July, when Joyce was calmed down.

She swung in a suspended bamboo chair in the crowded common room. Her braided hair hung like a bellpull, slick as if she'd combed it with margarine. I kissed her hello, hugged, and wouldn't let her go until she gave me a tentative shove. "I hope you don't think I'm mental." That was the first thing she said. "I'll have you know I've got both oars in the water."

She insisted Irene's bird had been an accident. She thanked me for the horoscopes I'd sent each week. She'd overreacted because she hadn't been ready to leave Eric and didn't know if she ever would be. "Has Eric called?"

"I don't know," I said. Joyce's lawyer had told us Eric was filing for divorce.

"Want to see my room?"

She shared it with three other women, whom she diagnosed as nuts. Joyce waved me onto the unmade bed and dragged over a chair. When another guest poked her nose in, I felt self-conscious, as if I were the patient.

"What does your doctor say?" I said.

"The sphinx?" she said. "Time. More time."

"What's wrong with you?"

Joyce shook her head. "What's wrong with *you*?"

I didn't know what to say. There was probably lots wrong. "What do you do every day?"

"Rotate," she said. "The earth turns around. I turn with it." She blew on a short fingernail. "You do, too, Delly."

I visited every afternoon after that. On the Saturdays I was supposed to see my real father, I told him I had to nurse Joyce. Joyce and I pretended we were tenants in a building with eccentric neighbours. We played Fish and tetherball. We lamented, with some other patients, the macaroni and the weather, but it didn't matter much. Joyce was right; we simply rode Earth.

One day Joyce and I were learning the bossa nova on the lawn, shuffling beside each other, when Rex beckoned from the veranda. He brought Joyce two books— one about a man sailing around the world by himself, and an atlas. She passed them to me.

"The P.N.E. opens Saturday," Rex said to Joyce. "If you're out soon, maybe we could go. Ride the Mad Mouse. Visit livestock."

"I don't think so," she said. "But thanks."

I examined the atlas. I felt sorry for both of them.

"I'm not anxious to see anybody, Rex."

"I understand," he said. "But feel free to call me, Joyce. Even for a cup of coffee. Call collect."

Joyce shook his hand at the electronic gate, then came back, and we lay on the lawn and watched the patients rumba. "I wish everybody would leave me alone," she said.

At supper, Robert asked if Joyce had cheered up during Rex's visit.

"Not really," I said.

"Why not?" Mum said.

"She cheered up when he left."

"She changes her mind so much," Mum said. "One day she hopes Eric's killed in a plane crash, and the next day she's depressed because they didn't have children. She doesn't know what she wants."

"She wants to be left alone," I said coldly. Robert looked up, suspecting my tone of voice. "Why don't you both leave her alone?"

Robert mumbled something about the peanut gallery and walked out the back door and turned on the water; he was soaking the grass. Mum waited.

"She's all right when she's with me," I said.

"She was with you when she got sick," Mum said. "She's a woman, Adele. She needs *somebody*."

"She just needs me," I said, trying not to cry.

Joyce was free to leave whenever she wanted and she chose to come home the day after Labour Day. Robert called in ill with flu to stay home and celebrate the reunion; Ray phoned to say Merry had an unusual headache. It was overcast, but we sat outside and broke open a bottle of domestic champagne. I'd memorized an original toast, but Mum clinked "To life" before I'd filled my glass. Then they gave Joyce a new bathing suit, one-piece, turquoise.

She was upstairs, seeing if it fit, when the bell rang, Groucho roused a bark, and I ran to the front door. An older guy wearing a Nehru jacket, trimmed in silver, cuddled a trumpet under his arm. "Is June home?" he said.

"Who are you?"

"Rudy, from the Musicians' Union. She said to drop by today."

"Everybody's in the yard," I said.

He walked around the corner of the house and Mum hailed him. I hurried inside.

The suit fit beautifully. "Should I model it?" Joyce said.

"I wouldn't. There's a trumpet player on the loose."

"Oh," she said. "Did they hire a band to welcome me back?"

We joined them on the patio. Mum served a platter of cold cuts, sliced rye, and gherkins, and they talked about live music in Canada. After Rudy had built his second open-face sandwich, he told us he was counting calories and newly single. His ex-wife, the ambitious vocalist, had transferred to Toronto.

I summoned Mum into the kitchen. "Did you invite that creep here today?"

"Yes," she said. "Rudolph's his name."

"Why today? For Joyce?"

"No, I'm thinking of forming a trio again."

"I bet."

Mum tugged my chin and I had to meet her eyes. "It's terrible to lose somebody close," she said. "I've been through it twice and I don't wish it on you, Adele. But when you're older you'll know." She let go of me, turned her back, and walked out to join everyone.

I watched through the window screen. Irene showed up with salad and Robert trotted by on his way to find another bottle of champagne. Mum stood listening to Rudy loudly outline the requisites for a hit: how the melody should be catchy, the chorus easy to remember, and how the lyrics should always be about falling in, or out of, love. Joyce was listless. She watched our dog, under Rudy's chair, flatten into sleep. Then she made a visor of her left hand. I saw my sister look up at the sky at something going awfully fast.

BOXING DAY

The morning after Christmas, I was in the kitchen picking at cold turkey and reading my new young-adult book. It was called *Milestone Summer* and it was all about a teenage girl named Judy, whose father's death plunges the family into a colourful, rather enviable poverty. She's forced to become a thrifty interior decorator after school and meets Kent, a catch, who's conceited and sails. There were misunderstandings, there were barbecue and pool parties, and I couldn't put it down. It was set in California.

My mother came in, scuffing her gift mules. "Is that your brother on the couch, I hope?" she asked.

"In person," I said.

"I didn't hear him come in," she said.

"I did."

"Late?"

"How late's late?"

"Two?"

"Yup."

"Under the influence?" she had to ask. I didn't say anything. "I guess he was, then," she said. She shook her head. "He won't be happy." She meant Robert. She'd married him even though he was twelve years her junior. Mum tucked a towel around the turkey and took it away. "You've polished off all the dark, Adele. You know that, don't you?"

"So *solly*," I said. "Like your mules?"

"They'll stretch," she said. "How's the book?"

"Judy had to miss the regatta and Kent stormed off in a huff."

"That's life," Mum said. She wandered out and I heard her in the living room patiently saying, "Raymond. Raymond. Raymond," until she gave up.

I placed the book face down and looked out the window. The yard glared. On the west coast, in Vancouver, we weren't accustomed to snow. Like a long spell of fair weather in summer, it was unusual, worthy of attention and respect, an omen. I watched a tabby cat follow its breath across the white crust. Every few feet, the cat sank, then kept perfectly still and waited for fate. I couldn't tell if it was scared stiff or smart.

Sleep took him away. Ray had a way of sleeping deep that made me jealous. His left eyebrow lifted in a kind of shrug and he smiled, as if privy to an epic starring his truly. I always wanted to see what he saw, do what he did, be where he was; our sisters, Irene and Joyce, were married and no longer fun.

I tickled my brother's nose with a strand of tinsel. He turned to the cushion. "Cut it out," he said. I brushed his cheek. "Cease and desist, or someone's going to hang from the tree, Adele." I stopped. He opened his eyes. "Merry X-mas," he said.

"That was yesterday," I said.

"Very funny."

"I'm not kidding," I said. "Starting with my stocking I got—"

Ray sat up. "My pants. Where are they?"

"La-Z-Boy," I said.

"No comments," he said. "Fetch."

I hopped up and brought his trousers over by a belt loop, so I wouldn't empty his pockets. He pulled them up and on. "Mumlet awake?" he asked. "The *hombre* of the house?"

"She's making the bed. Robert's making noise in the shower," I said. "Mum was worried about you. She called the RCMP to see if anybody who looked like you had died in an accident."

Ray shook his head. "I'm indestructible," he said. "Where's Dallyce?"

"Texas."

"The girl," he said.

"What girl?"

"I'm losing my marbles," he said. He threw on his sweater, tapped his pocket for nicotine, dug into his jacket, and pulled out car keys on a red rabbit's foot. "Grab your coat," he said. "Let's go quick."

At the drugstore Ray bought Mum everything Evening in Paris, the shebang; Robert, Old Spice deodorant and swizzle sticks, erotic ones, with buttocks and breasts; our sisters and their husbands, Black Magic chocolates, and opened them and ate all the ones with nuts when we got back to the Volkswagen. I chose Sea & Ski suntan lotion, which made you look Jamaican any season. It lasted longer than foundation. It didn't wash off. I wanted to fool kids at school and make them think I'd been somewhere. It was the only item Ray had to buy for full price.

On the way home from the mall Ray said, "So?"

"So?"

"So how's Mum doing? Okay?"

"I don't know," I said. "Ask her."

"You know the dirt. You're the only one home now. She and Robert still fight?"

I nodded.

"About?"

"You yesterday," I said. "How could you forget? You didn't even call."

"Long story." He braked for a yellow and we skidded over the traffic line into the intersection. A truck honked.

"Ice," I said, and he said, "Yeah, ice."

.   .   .

When Ray and I got back, a little whisper I'd never seen before, blond and maybe thirty, sat at the kitchen table absorbed by Judy's life. Her hands seemed too tiny to hold my book.

"Where's my mother?" Ray asked her.

"Don't know. Nobody was here when I got up," she said. She sounded as if she was coming down with something.

"They probably went next door for the open house," I said. "Then tonight we go to Irene's for turkey. It's her turn. We cooked yesterday. Joyce is having Christmas up at Eric's family's in Skookumchuck."

Ray and the lady stared at each other. Then she said, "Lose your manners somewhere?"

Ray planted a kiss in her direction, in air. "Dallyce, this is Adele," he said. "She's the baby of the family. Adele, Dallyce. She's my baby."

"Don't count on it," she said.

"So that's the lay of the land, eh?" He opened the fridge door, bent, and disappeared. "Where did you finally crash?"

"Down in the rec room," Dallyce said.

"Comfy?"

"The Ritz it's not."

"Dream of me?" he asked.

"A little hairy," she said, which made him peek at her over the door. I wasn't sure she'd heard him right.

"Come back down with me and I'll serenade you on the piano. Then you can giftwrap for me."

"Thanks, but no thanks," she said.

Ray cracked ice cubes into a tumbler and poured two fingers of rye. "You both know where I am," he said.

I took off my jacket and hung it over my chair. Dallyce and I looked at each other across the table, and then we heard the opening bars of "Moon River."

"My song," I said.

"He's not bad," she said.

"Yeah," I said. "You want coffee?"

Dallyce lit up. "Yes please, thanks."

I filled the kettle and plugged it in. "So have you known my brother very long?"

"Since Christmas." She folded the top of a page in my book and closed it. "You could say I found him in my stockings."

"Sugar?" I said. "Milk?"

"Both."

We waited for the kettle to whine. "So do you do anything? Work, I mean?"

"I teach."

"What?"

"I sub. Substitute. Science, French, P.E., you name it."

"Guidance?"

"Once I taught Guidance," she said.

"Guidance is for the birds," I said.

I poured the hot water and Dallyce came over to doctor the brew. She wore a striped mini-skirt with matching top, something Tarzan's Jane might toss on in the jungle first thing. I looked down. "Hey, you've got the same mules as Mum. My stepfather got her a pair."

"Oh," Dallyce said. "They're hers. Didn't feel like squeezing into my boots." She stirred her coffee. "Ray says your mother's visited the altar a few times, eh?"

"Three."

"Three times?"

"She's not exactly an Elizabeth Taylor," I said. "She's had it tough. It didn't work out with Ray's dad, and it didn't with mine."

"How's this one going?"

"Better."

"That's good." Dallyce put the mug down. "I was married once upon a time."

"Oh yeah?"

"Yeah. We got hitched on New Year's Day before the Polar Bear Swim. It was incredibly cold out, so we stayed in the car and watched all the crazy gooseflesh make a mad dash for the sea." Dallyce lifted an edge of the towel, tore off some turkey, and ate. She also picked dark. She said, "You might have to be crazy. It's not for everyone. The Polar Bear Swim."

When Mum and Robert trundled laughing up the driveway, Ray and Dallyce were still whispering and wrapping things in the rec room. I was reading, sprawled on the couch, under the tree lights. Robert, the big lug moose, stamped his boots on the front mat, then Mum the moose did. "It's below freezing," Robert said, opening the door. "Colder than a witch's tit."

"Here's my angel," Mum said. "Right under the tree."

"That's no angel," Robert said boisterously. "That's the brat."

"Don't call her that." Mum used her mock hurt voice.

"Why not?" Robert said. "That's what she is—the original brat."

"How was it?" I asked. "The open house?"

Mum slid off her coat and hung it up. "Nice to see the snooty neighbours. I guess."

"Once a year is once too much." Robert lowered himself into the La-Z-Boy. "You wouldn't believe it, Adele. What the Strachans did? Should I tell her what the stupid Strachans did, Beauty?"

Mum floated back in. "Oh, I don't think she's really interested, hon."

"Sure she is."

"Not really." I pointed to my book. "Judy and Kent are on the brink."

"Hey." Robert stood, crossed to the couch, and crouched by me, his breath in my face. If I struck a match, the air between us would have lit. "And what are Judy and Kent on the brink of? Love? Hate? Wild sex? All three? Will there be a happy ending? Will anybody die? Who did it?"

"Don't torture her, Bob," Mum said.

"I'm not. Am I torturing you, brat?"

"Yup."

Robert made a sad face, grabbed the last handful of peanuts from the dish on the coffee table, and sat back down.

"Where'd Ray get to?" Mum said. "His car's still—?"

"Rec room," I said. "He's got a guest."

"Who?" Robert jumped up again.

"A schoolteacher."

"A schoolteacher!" Robert said. "Not a parole officer?"

"A schoolteacher," I said.

Robert strode into the hall and bellowed, "Raymond, bring your teacher up and introduce her to your parents."

"He's irrepressible," I said.

Mum looked at me from across the room. "It wouldn't hurt for you to take an interest in what he has to say," she said gently. "After all, who's keeping a roof over your head? Who's putting presents under the tree? And," she said pointedly, "peanuts in the dish?"

"I was only reading," I said.

"Who provided what you're buried in?" she said. "You know, he would give the shirt off his back for you kids. Does anybody ever think it hurts me to see him ignored?"

I closed my eyes. In the hallway, my brother introduced Dallyce to Robert. "My mother seems to have vanished," Ray said. "She tapped her magic mules together and went away."

"No, here I am," Mum said, and cleared her throat. "I'm right here."

Ray was ages in the upstairs john and Robert was verbal. He was warmed up. "Well, Dallyce. June— Ray's mother—and me—"

"I'm Adele's mother, too," Mum interrupted.

"Yes," Robert said, "June is Ray and Adele's mother, and since we're being technical, Irene and Joyce's mother, and what the hell, she's everybody's mother. Happy now?" he said.

"Happy," she said.

"Good. All right. What I was starting to say, Dallyce, was that June and I are what you could call a love match. I've been through a couple of tragic marriages I won't go into tonight. June here has suffered through two. Ray Senior, her first husband, busted her heart running off with a Calgary telephone operator, which would be the polite thing to call her. And Adele's dad . . ." Here Robert glanced at me across the rec room. "Well, how would you tell the story, Adele?"

"I don't know," I said.

He looked at my mother. "How would you describe it, Sweeter than Honey?"

Mum twisted the glass in her hand. She looked tired. She needed lipstick. "Well, he didn't know how to show affection. You've probably met men like that, Dallyce."

"Sure," Dallyce said softly. "One or two."

"With him it was always work, work, work," Mum said.

Robert got up to fix himself another drink. He was tall, with a voice big and capable as nature. He lowered it now. "Honey, in fact, wouldn't it be fair to say Adele might not even be here if you hadn't (pardon my being crass, Dallyce) got down to brass tacks? Correct me if I'm wrong."

Dallyce studied me hard, as if I were coming and going before her very eyes. My mother nodded and said, "That's true." Then she looked at me and added, "But I would have had you anyway, Adele. Nothing could have stopped me."

"Of course," Dallyce murmured.

Robert went on. "June hoped the baby would save the marriage, you see."

"Right," Dallyce said.

"Now let's drop it," Mum said. "It's Boxing Day."

Ray came back in. "Why's everybody so serious? It's time to—" and he sang, "*Jingle bell, jingle bell, jingle bell rock.*"

"Your stepfather—" Dallyce began.

"Bob, please," Robert said. "And let me compliment you on your good taste, Ray." He gave a little nod Dallyce's way.

Dallyce nodded back. "Bob here was explaining how he and your mother got together and that marriage as an institution really works."

"Humbug," Ray said, making me laugh. "Let's party."

"Isn't he something?" Mum said to Dallyce.

I passed around the chips and garlic dip. Dallyce took only a few, because she was on the mistletoe diet. Robert said she didn't need to lose. He said if Ray poured mercury into her he could use her to tell the temperature. She said, "Your parents are terrific. They really are the Hosts with the Mostest."

I picked up the phone on the sixth or seventh ring. "What's going on over there?" Irene shouted. "My bird's drying out in the oven. Peter's starving."

"Ray's here," I said.

"Is he all right? Where'd he blow in from?"

"Nowhere," I said. "He's okay."

My sister paused. "Were there words? From you know who?"

"No," I said. "Ray brought a girl."

"Who?"

"A teacher."

"Smart move," Irene said. "Well, round everybody up, pup, and get over here. We'll wait for you. Tell Ray to drive carefully, there's a lot of roadblocks, and don't you ride with him. Go with Mum." She paused. "What's that?"

"Everybody's singing carols."

"Who's everybody?"

"Mum, Ray, Robert, and Dallyce."

"Her name's Dallyce?"

"Yup."

"And what are you doing? Nose in a book? Don't say yup."

I hung up, and Mum came upstairs and poked her head around the corner. "Who was it?"

"Irene. She's holding the turkey for us."

"We better get going." Mum leaned closer. "Dallyce seems like a nice gal, doesn't she?"

"She's all right," I said.

"You don't like her?"

"I didn't say that," I said. "I said she's all right."

"Her skirt's short, though," Mum said. "Isn't it?" Then she rested her hand against my forehead. "Are you okay, hon?"

"A–1," I said.

She went back down and I went up to the bathroom. I locked the door and took off my blue corduroy jumper and white blouse and slip and underpants and navy-blue knee socks. I clipped my bangs back with Mum's bobby pins. I gave the Sea & Ski a good shake, unscrewed the cap, poured lotion into my palm, and applied it thinly and evenly. It was cool. Across my forehead and cheeks, around my nose and lips and eyes, down my neck and shoulders and below, on any bit of me that might ever show. It was like getting into someone else's skin. I waited a few minutes for it to dry.

.   .   .

On the other side of the hill we lived on, there was only a sprinkle of snow. Enough to keep the plastic reindeer, strutting across lawns and roofs, and sleighs from being ridiculous. It was already pitch dark. Mum wiped the windshield clear with her glove and Ray's VW taillights blinked at us.

"She looks stupid," Robert said.

"She doesn't look stupid," Mum said. "Why do you keep saying that? She looks like she's just stepped out of a play. She looks made up."

"She looks stupid," Robert said. "Tell me why you did it."

"Don't say again I look stupid," I said.

"Well," he said, "you do."

"Enough," Mum said.

"She does. I'm just curious to know why a half-bright eleven-year-old would do such a stupid thing."

"I did it," I said, "because I wanted to pretend I'd been somewhere else."

"Oh," Robert said. "India?"

I didn't answer.

"Is this meant to criticize me as the breadwinner? Because we can't afford to take holidays like your friends?" Robert asked.

"You're going too far," Mum said.

"Am I?"

"Change the subject, Bob."

Ray made a quick left, Robert followed, then Ray picked up the speed.

"That Dallyce seems pretty nice," Mum said. "Down-to-earth. Maybe she'll be the one."

"A teacher," Robert said. "He probably didn't meet her in the pub."

I piped up. "They met at a mutual friend's."

We drove in silence. Ray made another left, and then we did. The road was dark and bordered by open fields. I remembered my father had taken me to the pony rides there when I was little. I'd sat on the back of Hi-Yo, Silver, the oldest, most polite pony in captivity, and Dad had led us around, around, and around the winding sawdust path until the pony's bedtime. Now it was a new development.

Robert's signal kept ticking after the turn.

"Ray won't keep a girl like that, honey. A teacher and all. He's got to really shape up. Lay off the booze."

"You think she's better than him?"

He sighed loudly. "Why do you always twist my words, dear?" he asked.

"Am I twisting them, dear?"

"I think so, dear," he said. "What do you say in the back seat?"

"I'm not here," I said. Ray seemed to be going faster and leaving us behind. His taillights shrunk in the distance.

"Sometimes I get the feeling everyone's against me in

this family," Robert said. "I really get that feeling." His voice shook.

"Here we go," Mum said. "Deck the halls. Tra la la la la. And do you know the feeling I get, dear?"

"No."

"I get the feeling you could really go for a young girl like that. Wearing bare legs up to there."

Robert glanced over at her. "Take that back," he said.

"Up to heaven," Mum said.

"You'll take that back," he said. Robert laid on the gas and we shot up the road.

Ray slowed, and signalled, and pulled into my sister's driveway. He was unfolding himself from the car, one foot on the ground, as we zipped by Irene's twinkling home. Dallyce must have been waiting for him to jog around and open her door. For a second, I could see what he saw. The Plymouth going dangerously fast; two ghosts in the front seat, my shadow behind.

"Take it back," Robert yelled, and pointed the car at a tall cedar on the side of the road. There was no way we weren't going to hit. We were going to hit. We were going to hit. Off pavement, on the gravel shoulder, the car sang, as Robert edged the wheel and pressed the brakes. When the car stopped, our bodies kept travelling forward, then we snapped the few inches back into ourselves.

In the car we sat still. No one was hurt. The night was back outside us and the brights lit up the ice. The gauges on the dash glowed blue. He stared straight ahead, breathing rough. In that big cold quiet, she turned to him and kissed him, and kissed again, until she kissed him into kissing, kissing her back, until I couldn't hear the in, out, in again of our breath.

K L I N G O N S

In 1960, Mum fell for Robert Kiely and began their affair. She met him secretly at White Rock, a beach down by the United States border, where not too many people went because it was beside a railroad track, rather rocky, and out of the way. She carted me along. He brought his daughter, Louise. Mum said, "She's such a dearness."

Louise was my age exactly, six. She was prettier, with a parade of faces: pink lips pressed into a shocked *Oh*; her furtive squirrel's glance; an expression that was above-it-all, eyes sideward, as if listening to a voice far-off and more important. Whenever she took a sip, she grew a mustache of muddy root beer. She also wore a yellow bathing suit with a pleated skirt and Robert called her his walking sunflower. I wanted to boss her.

It was hot and overcast. Robert stooped to take our hands and we travelled over the wet sand with him. He said, "Tide's out to hell and gone. Tide's damn near to Japan," and I had the feeling we might all walk there together if it didn't rain or thunder.

Louise showed off her float while Robert gave pointers on mine. Whenever the current carried her away, he tugged her to him by a toe juicy red with polish. Soon she wandered back to the Hudson's Bay blanket, held her knees, and gazed out at the sea; perhaps waiting for a big interesting wave to arrive. I saw Mum fuss, rubbing Noxzema on her. "I'm tuckered out," I said to Robert.

We changed behind towels. Robert held Louise's while she stepped into clean panties. Her beach towel had a whale shaking fins with a happy goldfish. Mum held mine—plain orange—and it gaped. Louise giggled; she pointed at some bare part of me, and furious, I kicked sand at Mum and exposed even more of myself. Finally we were in shorts, fussy blouses, socks, and running shoes, with straw coolie hats on.

We pretended to be Siamese cats. We meowed and rubbed up against a respective parent's legs until we started hissing at each other, hunched. Robert said, "Behave." He was still wearing his bikini trunks and Mum snapped a lot of pictures of him with the Brownie. When he slid her straps down for a shot, Louise and I pulled them back up, matching them with her white marks. He didn't find that funny.

It was my idea that Louise and I visit the railroad track and play a game. I showed her how to lie down on the wooden crosstie. I lifted my hands high over my head and pretended they were roped at the wrists; I crossed my legs at the ankles. I called "Hailp" in a soft, unworried, Southern accent I'd heard in a cartoon. "Hailp," I said again, and she lay down, fitting as neatly as me, her wrists and ankles also invisibly bound, and we stared into each other's eyes and said, "Hailp. Hailp."

We heard the whistle. The rails, full of summer heat, shook. Neither of us budged. We just smiled bigger at each other and chirped, "Hailp." I know that when my mother heard the locomotive she instinctively checked and, when she didn't see us, tore up the slope to the track, Robert behind her.

When I looked past Louise and saw an engine—big, close, the single lit eye against the day—I froze. I only remember Robert yanking my arms, and my swinging up and hitting hard against his hairy chest. He knocked the wind out. The train chugged slowly by. Under the *ding ding ding ding* a man yelled, "You dummy assholes." Mum was on the other side. She hugged Louise and cradled her. "Daddy," Louise whimpered.

At a picnic table, Robert turned her over his knee and spanked her until she started to choke and Mum put a hand on his shoulder and said, "Bob." He volunteered to deal with me, but Mum delivered her usual tongue-lashing. She also called me Miss Simpleton. On the way home, before we got to the lot where Mum's car was parked, we stopped for soft ice cream. Louise asked her dad to please sing the song he'd made up, and in a silly voice he went, "Every leetle breeze zeems do whisper Louise. De boys in de trees zeem do twitter Louise." She licked with her faraway look. When I asked him to make up one for me, Mum said she couldn't think of one for Adele. Then Robert started, "The farmer in the dell, the farmer in the dell," and Mum joined in, "Heigho! the derry oh." Louise and I sat far apart and listened.

Louise's mother died from lung cancer in 1967. "She smoked like a fish," Robert said, and debated with my mum, whom he'd married, about attending the funeral: she didn't want him to. Then he said he'd make up his own mind and decide not to, and took a hike up Burnaby Mountain. He'd never hiked. He came home late and fell drunk out of a cab. Mum didn't say anything; she'd learned the hard way not to comment on his actions. Instead, she talked about poor Louise, denied the father who loved her by a vengeful mother, and now she'd lost that mother, vengeful or not. An aunt was appointed Louise's guardian.

Then there was a call. It came down to this: Louise wanted to be with her dad.

It was agreed she'd move in the weekend before Easter vacation. Mum and Robert hoped the ten days would give her time to grieve and to adjust to us before transferring into a strange class—mine.

On Good Friday, the night before Robert picked Louise up, I dreamed Mum died by falling into a volcano. She'd been walking bossily along, her hair in rollers under a chiffon kerchief, and then she suddenly wasn't talking. She was gone. I crawled to the edge of the cone and looked down at the beautiful sea of lava. I looked and looked. Dream days later, starved, when I still hadn't found her, I thought, *Now there's nobody to love me*. I woke up with an unidentifiable ache. I wanted to call out; I wanted her to bring graham wafers and milk and sit. But I stayed in bed, eyes absorbing the night, and I glanced around the now half-empty room I was going to share.

It was pouring rain when they arrived. From behind the drape, I watched her alight from the car. She didn't resemble a poor child; under a bright umbrella, she chattered away as if it were Christmas. Robert chuckled as the trunk lid yawned, and he started carting her clan of matched luggage. I could see Louise and I were no longer the same height. I was taller, the giantess of grade seven, while she was petite, frail in a paisley shirtdress, and allowed to wear fishnets.

Boys would truly like her. Probably even Mike Beckett, whom I respected as a speller, revered as a short love god, and who'd hit me with a rock in a snowball back in February. Mum had dispensed ice and consolation by saying M.B. must think highly of me. In her book, boys were cruel only to girls they liked.

Louise appeared at the front door. As soon as our eyes

met, I was intimidated and despised her slightly. She beat me to a Hi. Without wiping her feet, she stepped inside.

That first week the four of us did things as a team and ate big dinners. Louise seemed deaf when Mum spoke, and didn't talk or look her way, but I didn't hold it against her. She may have noticed I didn't hang around her amusing father, who'd dubbed Louise and me Kling-ons, after a race of ugly aliens from a warfaring planet on TV.

In Chinatown one night, Louise tugged Robert's finger and he belched and her face exploded in a smile, sud-denly like his, and I thought, *We're being invaded*; but farther down the block, while Robert explained the cause of a mirage, Louise interrupted to say, "You know you're tall enough to be a model, Adele?" and I sort of liked her.

Later in our beds in my crowded room, we talked candidly about when we'd been children. She said her father and mother had prayed on their knees before bed and had never argued. I volunteered that my real dad had had a prostate operation.

Louise sat up on her elbow. "Remember White Rock?"

"Yeah."

"The train?"

I nodded.

"Know when my dad saved you?"

"Yeah."

"I thought he loved you more than me."

"Really?" I said. "How retarded. Robert grabbed me and Mum saved you because they were so madly in love then, they didn't want the other one to mope forever if their kid got killed." I sat up on my elbow, too. "When he heard you wanted to live here?"

"Yeah."

"He cried."

"Really?" She pondered. "He was sad?"

"No. Happy. No lie."

Louise lay back down. If she remembered anything else, she didn't mention it.

The next night I held a pajama party in Louise's honour and invited my five closest girl friends of the month. Penny didn't want to sleep over because she was afraid she'd say *mother* or *death*; she thought she'd have an hysterical fit, something she was prone to and good at, but her parents needed to get out and forced her to come.

We danced the Swim to Louise's 45s. She watched the records spin and made sure my needle didn't scratch them. She sullenly perused *Seventeen*, then went up and watched TV, snuggled by Robert. Mum guided her back to the rec room, gave me the look, and left. Nobody liked Louise. But while she brushed her teeth, I took Judith and Lynn aside and commanded them to befriend her. She emerged from the bathroom and then they all miraculously hit it off. The sleeping bags radiated out, their three heads met in the center, and Louise held court. She spoke in a luxurious whisper while Penny, Gail, Caroline, and I played cribbage.

Louise went upstairs again. She'd been back only a few seconds when I heard a gasp and our group turned to look. Judith stared at something in Louise's hand, and Lynn shut her eyes. "What?" I said. Then louder, "What?"

Louise covered it, like you capture a bug with your hand. "You don't want to see."

"Show me."

She made her squirrel face, hesitated, and then passed a small black-and-white photograph. The lady was naked above the waist; she cupped her breasts and offered them up. Her nipples were hard as pen erasers. She seemed to be perched on a Queen Anne chair identical to the one in our living room. She smiled right at me, but her eyes were deeply ashamed. It was my mum, young, from years ago. I closed my eyes, too. I thought I heard Louise say, "My mother didn't die from cancer."

Nobody said anything. Caroline went white. Penny did not collapse, although I wished hard. All the oxygen in the area had been used up; my lungs couldn't find any. "I think it's time to go to sleep," I said. "I'm turning out the light now and I don't think anybody better talk."

The rec room was silent the rest of the night, except when one girl snuffled into her pillow and when Robert poked his nose in and said, "Keep it down to a dull roar, eh?" In the morning, none of us—Louise, my friends, ex-friends, or me—admitted hunger, and Robert drove one quiet contingent home, Mum the other. They didn't ask. Mum believed in letting life blow over.

I did not talk to Louise; she did not converse with me. We walked to school, one slightly ahead of the other, then the one behind seizing the lead. Mrs. Rude introduced her to the class: "This is Louise Kiely, Adele Nordstrom's stepsister," and suggested a tour of our exceptional facilities.

I showed the new bilingual library, the nurse's cave where the nurse smoked herself grey when she wasn't off sick, and the old gym. I opened doors and let them bang shut. In her Hush Puppies, she followed my deafening penny loafers into the girls' changing room, the linoleum slippery with talc, the scent suffocating, the mirrors losing steam. When her back was turned, with a ferocity I'd never before experienced, I shoved her into a damp shower stall.

Louise cowered against the tiles. I put my hand on the tap. My mission was to set her straight and say her mother wasn't a saint, leave my mum alone, and, more than anything, to tell her about her father—the dirty jokes that embarrassed me, the yelling, the door he'd kicked a hole through. But I didn't speak.

She was so little. She looked at my grip on the hot-water faucet and started to cry. She bent at the knees and sank down to the drain, next to a bit of white soap, and she was shrinking. She looked absolutely alone in the world.

I sank down, too. I sat beside her, not touching. I said, "I'm sorry about your mum."

We both cried silently. The buzzer rang for recess. Outside, banshees waged hopscotch and skipped. We stayed in the dark stall a while longer, then proceeded like those synchronized twins in films on hygiene to the sinks, splashed our faces, wiped them dry with a rough paper towel, and sat on a changing bench to wait. When recess was over we went back wearing big wet spots on our dresses.

Not long after, she ran away. She left the picture. I have it still.

I did not see Louise again until one spring night in 1973. I came home from waitressing, pulled up behind an unfamiliar car in the driveway, and heard Robert pontificating. When I ventured out to the patio, I saw their faces and then focused on Mum's troll, the one she called our Guard Dwarf, by the rosebush.

"Welcome, stranger," Louise said. She leaned next to her father, elbows nicking, at the table.

"Come by Mum, Coconut." Mum waved at me and patted the bench. I straddled it on her side.

Robert poured a glass of wine and said, "Louise just landed here. She's catching us up."

"I missed everybody," Louise said. "I missed Dad.

Having a sister. A mum." She looked apologetically at my mother. I sensed a moment between them, then Mum bit into an extremely crisp potato chip. "Sorry," she said nervously. "Loud chip."

Louise smiled quickly and went on. She'd wed last summer, Felix deserted her three days later in a cottage on a Gulf island, and the marriage was annulled; she'd been pregnant, miscarried, then there were complications and her tubes were tied. Her aunt disowned her. Louise relayed this without a hint of self-pity. She told this without any expression at all, as if it might have happened to somebody else.

"For having been through the mill"—Robert gripped Louise's hand—"my daughter looks damn good."

"You're like me and your dad," Mum said to her. "The school of hard knocks."

"Prep school," Louise said. "Anyway, the past is water under the bridge." She paused. "Maybe someday I'll adopt." She got up, took a napkin from the barbecue stand, and held it against her face. Robert went and hugged her. Mum started gathering glasses and nudged me, but I stayed put and studied Louise. She wore flares, a peasant blouse, and platforms. Barefoot we would be the same height again, medium, neither here nor there; she was still thin—a gasp for a waist—and her bangs and garden of scarlet nails grew long. It was hard to believe we were both nineteen, and she three months younger.

Over Robert's shoulder Louise said, "So, Adele? Breaking hearts?" They let go of each other and Robert blew out the flames.

"A few," I said.

"When a guy winks," Robert announced to Louise and the neighbours, "she runs a hundred miles an hour. The other way."

"She types a hundred miles." Mum came back out with a wet cloth and wiped the table. "She won an award. Adele, what was the name of it again?"

"The typing award."

"Congratulations," Louise said. She sounded earnest. "Look," she said. "Tomorrow night I'm having a wingding and why don't you come?" She claimed she'd invited some super nice folk.

"Sounds fun," Robert said. "Maybe I'll show up, too."

"We've got church," Mum reminded him. "In the morning?"

"Actually I'm working," I said.

Robert seemed hurt, which Mum immediately noticed. "Go after your shift, Adele," she said. "It'll do you good. Leave us big kids alone for a night."

Mum and Robert walked Louise to her car and I moved mine out of her way. "Come," she called to me. "I'd like to know you better." She honked and I watched her take off down the street. In the rearview, her taillights looked like ladybugs hanging on.

The next night I went to Louise's after work, around eleven. It was dead quiet. A swag lamp burned in the duplex window and somebody sat on the bottom step of the cement porch. "It's you," Louise said. She was wearing a leotard top and a long skirt cut out of grandmotherly curtains. "Pull up a chair."

I sat down beside her. "Where is everybody?"

"Gone." She didn't appear devastated; she seemed preoccupied, depressed in a sophisticated manner, and pulled a joint out of a pouch and lit it. "Smoke?"

"I've never."

"Won't hurt. It'll relax you." She inhaled, held her breath, exhaled, and delicately passed it. "Here."

I conscientiously puffed. Not far away, stevedores worked graveyard and boxcars bumped at the docks, dumping the guts of Canada into boats bound for Asia. She eventually spoke. "Was it nice growing up with two parents?" she asked.

"Not really," I said.

"Why?"

"Used to fight a lot."

"Still?"

"No." I didn't add that people often have to speak to each other before they can officially fight.

We finished the smoke together. "In Roman, my ex's name, Felix, means happy." She hugged herself, then slipped out of her shoes and headed over to a bush by the basement window where she turned a faucet. A sprinkler whooshed on and spun. Water sparkled in the streetlight. "Come on," she said. For some reason obscure at the time, I shed my clogs and followed her over the brush of cool grass. She walked very slowly through the arc of water and I followed, then she turned and walked through again and I followed, and we did this until we noticed we were soaked and cold.

One Saturday morning Louise phoned me at the last minute to go skiing with her up at Whistler. We'd become, if not exactly friends, companions. Weekends we danced at pubs, where she picked up men for both of us. (The extent of my lust was a kiss and sips from the same glass. I was a virgin and not convinced I could make walls shake and men tremble, or ever come as loudly and vivaciously as she claimed to do.) Other times, she dropped over to Mum's for dinner; Ray, Joyce, and Irene all liked her, which pleased Robert no end. And many nights I virtuously stared down the TV and Mum slept on the chesterfield, flirting with a snore, while father and daughter whispered late in another room. Robert even popped over to Louise's to perform manly errands—lift something, hang a picture straight. I sensed a wrong had been righted.

This particular day Louise was in a lousy mood, hung over, I assumed, and sped in silence up the long road. There were no lines at the chair lift. We plunked down, kept our tips up, and swung our bare legs over the treetops. It must have been seventy degrees.

I hadn't ever skied; she'd had lessons. I followed her down the bunny incline several times, mimicking her form, falling, then we broke for lunch. My boots pinched, I was burned on my nose and knees, but she pushed me to try a tougher run.

We caught the lift to the top. Louise lit up. "What do you think of Doris?" she asked.

"Doris who?"

"Doris in the choir with Dad and Mum."

"Doris whose husband croaked?" Louise nodded. "Not much. Why?"

"You sitting down?" she said. "She's in love with Dad." Louise hung her head back and looked at the wire bearing us up. "She wants him to move in."

I was silent. For a minute I knew life without Robert. Then I remembered. "Does Mum know?"

"He's telling her today," Louise said. She looked upset. "That's why he wanted you out."

We got to the top, but when I skied away from the lift my legs buckled and I fell. When I stood, I couldn't stay up. It was as if I'd received an electric shock and my leg muscles jerked, independently violent. Then it spread to my arms and hands and I couldn't grip the poles. My teeth chattered. I got frightened; then Louise did, too. "We're going down," she said.

They stopped the lift and we went back in a parade of empty chicken chairs. Skiers going up gave us funny looks. When we landed, I leaned on her, then stood on my own and walked well. "Let's go home," I said.

We arrived at Mum and Robert's just past dinner. Both cars were in the driveway. Nobody drank on the patio, the curtains were drawn and the house locked. I took out my key. The kitchen table still wore breakfast: cereal box, eggshell, cold buttered toast, and the lidless teapot.

"Mum?" I called.

"Dad," Louise said.

I went upstairs. She was right behind me. Their bedroom door was closed. I knocked. No answer.

Louise nearly socked her fist through. "Roberto?"

I opened the door and we went in. They were lying side by side on top of the bed. For a second, I thought they were dead. They were utterly still, but not asleep, and staring at the ceiling. They were dressed—Mum wore a black blouse Robert had given her birthdays ago, and Robert was bare-chested but wearing slacks. Mum was under an afghan. She moved her eyes to look at Louise and me, as if she hadn't strength to turn her head. She was terribly frail. Robert also seemed under the weather. He couldn't quite meet Louise's gaze and didn't acknowledge that I'd entered the room. I knew that if Robert's and my eyes met, he ran the risk of being vaporized. Louise sat on her father's side of the bed. I settled by Mum and kissed her cheek, which was cold, and folded her hand, cold, in mine.

"Guess you know the story, eh?" Robert said.

"The world knows," Mum said.

"Oh, Beauty," he said. "The world does not."

We were all quiet and then Louise said, "I'll make some dinner." She got up. "Dad, come with me, why don't you?"

Robert followed her downstairs. I moved over to his side, punched up a pillow, and sat there with my knees pulled up. It was still hot from his body; it felt as if I were sitting on top of him. I rested my hand on Mum's shoulder. "Is monster leaving?" I asked.

She shook her head. "He says he doesn't know what got into him." Her sentences arrived one at a time. "We've been married going on eight now. He's not going to throw it away. He doesn't want to hurt you kids. Don't call him monster."

"He is one."

She reached for a glass of cranberry juice and sipped. She put it back. "I couldn't think of singing at choir practice tonight. But I bet she's there. I don't understand her. We always got on good with her and Nat. He was a tenor. I don't understand how she could do this."

"Robert should see an eminent psychiatrist."

"I know," she said. "Maybe I should, too. Somebody famous."

Louise and Robert murmured and banged things in the kitchen.

"You know I love you, Mum."

She patted my leg. "Coconut."

Louise and I took off after the scrambled eggs, their second grim breakfast. I hadn't wanted to leave them alone together—they were too quiet for my comfort—but Louise was antsy. She'd found out where Doris lived and wanted to pay her respects. We parked up the street and rang the doorbell of the basement suite in a split-level.

When there wasn't a response, I lifted the welcome mat and Louise checked under the drooping fuchsia in the hanging basket and found luck. She unlocked the door and we waltzed in like houseguests.

It was fixed up cosy and neat. Humbugs in a goblet, quaint texts on trivets, and a calendar predicting a full and busy future: doctor, chiro, potluck, choir.

I found myself in the bedroom. You could still smell cologne in the air, Je Reviens, same as my mother's. On the dresser, there was a portrait of thin, fiftyish Doris, her late husband, and a quartet of pale adults with successful ears. Propped against this were wallet snaps of abominable red newborns. There was also a picture of the United Church choir taken during one of last Easter's three SRO services. I'd seen a copy at home. I picked the photo up and found them before God in their places, in their white gowns, mouths open vulnerably wide. They all shone with that radiant belief: Doris, Mum, Robert. He'd told Louise he prayed every Sunday that God would take him before Mum, so he wouldn't be left in the world without her. Louise had believed him. We all needed to believe something—even that the widow was to blame. Then I heard Louise quietly dismantling Doris's kitchen. I placed all the photos face down on the throw rug. I opened a drawer full of slippery nighties, pulled it out, turned it over, and spilled. Then I did another. Louise and I worked diligently. We didn't break anything. We emptied. We took things apart. We were a team. We were blood. When we left Doris's suite a half hour later, we took nothing. Her house was flipped totally upside down.

The next day we drove to the water. It was gorgeous, sunny, so of course it was impossible to park at Jericho, Locarno, or Spanish Banks, and we kept going until we were near the cliffs at Point Grey, below the university, at Wreck Beach. It was nude. "Game?" asked Louise.

I stripped.

We spread our beach towels by a log and Louise introduced herself to a hunk Dane right away. His English was excellent, and everything else seemed pretty tiptop, too. She said, "And this is my twin sister. We almost double-suicided when we were kids." He didn't think we looked related.

The guy professed to know a lot about the Nordic occult, but described Louise's aura using the usual details. When she inquired, he looked in my direction and said I didn't have one, perhaps because I was a young soul and had never lived before. "Not to worry," he said. "You are living now."

I could not get comfortable. When I opened my eyes, I saw too much and couldn't stop looking. Some people were very ugly naked. When I shut my eyes, I was seen.

Louise finally told Knut to hike. We both sat up and watched his snowy lean cheeks stride away. She asked, "You all right?"

"I don't know," I said. I was crying.

"Let's see your hand," she said.

It shook. I thought she was going to read my palm—

predict sex with Prince Charles, royal quints—but she simply clasped it in her own. We sat holding hands until she stood, and I got up, too, then walked over the sand into the warm water and went under. For those wonderful seconds, we'd never been born.

H E A R T B E A T

met Bill when I was doing
research for my graduate thesis in cultural anthropology
at Columbia. He was studying galaxies. I loved him for
his vision and ability to see the distance; I wasn't sure
what he saw in me. After living together for eight
months, we seldom enjoyed the peace or lust we'd known
before splitting the rent.

One night in April, while Bill and I fought about his
long hours gawking in a topless bar, I gathered all the
fruit in our apartment. Anything juicy, easily bruised:
apples, bananas, a kiwi. I threatened to quit my pro-
gram and spend nights at International House until I
could find a ride and return to Canada.

"Why are you packing all the fruit, Adele?" Bill sat at
the kitchen table, his feet propped on a chair. He wore
sweatpants, a turtleneck, and a fuzzy toque, all of which

kept him warm on cold evenings. A biography of Galileo was open on his lap. Bill looked reliable: a man for home and yard.

"In case I get hungry. It's a long drive north," I said.

"I don't believe you."

"I don't care."

The truth was, Bill and I often shared fruit after making love, and I didn't want him performing this intimacy with anybody else. I could imagine myself skulking away and another woman arriving. They'd make rigorous New York love, and afterwards Bill might feed her the firm Bings we'd so carefully picked. (Even though cherries were scarce, my imagination easily supplied them.) Or they'd share a plush wedge of watermelon and she'd spit the little black seeds onto his stomach in her casual way, aiming for his bellybutton, missing. Incautious, they'd nibble the white on the rind. He'd never notice my absence.

"Let me get this straight. You're leaving but you're only packing apples?"

"Right," I said. "I don't want you offering them to anybody else."

Bill looked down at his lap, then back at me. He seemed very tired. "Please trust me," he said.

I closed the door on him and intended to walk into the night. I ended up in the communal laundry down the hall. Nobody else was there; it was after midnight. I sat cross-legged on a dryer and listened for the reassuring scuff of his flip-flops along the corridor. But heard only soft laughter, the striking of a match, from somebody else's rooms.

I bit into the apples and chewed faces: eyes and lips of red peel, oddly pared smiles. I watched the pulp surrounding these strange features turn brown. Then I went back.

Bill still sat at the table. His book was turned to the same page. "Come sit on my knee, Adele," he said, and I did.

When my mother and stepfather called long distance the next morning, to invite us to join them in Florida, Bill and I had made old promises again and were toasting bread for BLTs.

They believed it was the best graduation gift they could offer—two weeks with the three most important people in my life in a state I'd never visited. Their other reasons: I deserved a holiday after college, before the future; they hadn't seen me in ages. In other words, they hadn't ever seen my boyfriend, Bill. Except in snaps.

From my chattering letters, they didn't guess Bill and I argued definitions of fidelity. They knew about the weekend jaunt to Martha's Vineyard, how it hadn't rained, how we steamed our own mussels on the beach facing Chappaquiddick and paced widow's walks. They didn't know about our real life and how I worried Bill was meeting a lover at the library near certain call numbers. Or how pensive I was when he danced salsa, two songs in a row, with the ecstatically married secretary from the Astronomy Department.

What they didn't know wouldn't hurt them. Sometimes I was sure Bill thought that about me. I hoped Florida would effect a cure: the sun and sleep and privacy.

Mum and Bill burned on the very first morning. Bonded, they compared noses, shoulders, and kneecaps, and trudged back to the rooms for cold teabags. "Takes the sting out, Bill," my mother said.

Robert and I continued to tan silently on the beach; the scent of coconut hung like a net. I listened to the Gulf of Mexico and heard children shouting, angrily, far away. I stretched in the direction of Texas.

"So, Adele." Robert's voice seemed to come from nowhere, from the Gulf. "Bill studied astronomy."

"That's right."

"And what's he going to pursue?"

I considered answers. Then chose to say, "Research. He wrote his final paper on asteroids and the atmosphere."

He didn't say anything for a while. I glanced at him; he was staring out at the water, and I saw, from the angle of his head, that he was watching a small trawler.

"So he's serious about space, eh?"

"Yes."

He nodded, then looked at me. "You should turn."

I shifted onto my stomach and felt the cool wind brush my back and legs. The conversation seemed over; Robert decided to go into the water. He shuffled his feet in the shallow depth to intimidate any drowsing devilfish. Then he started a strong crawl towards some point he had fixed upon.

Later that afternoon, the four of us drove in the rental car to the J. N. "Ding" Darling National Wildlife Refuge. The car smelled of Noxzema and Robert's skin bracer. Too late for the escorted tour, we drove miles on dirt roads through mangroves, stopping at outlooks.

"What are we looking for?" Mum demanded. "There's a bird," she said, pointing at the sky.

Robert, wearing binoculars and a movie camera, read all the signs. "Alligators."

"I'm waiting in the car," Mum said, then vanished. She called from the rolled-down window, "Watch where you're going, Adele."

We explored the swamp for almost half an hour. Every gator we discovered was a drifting stick. But Bill spotted eleven geckos, and we saw a spoonbill grubbing under a gumbo-limbo tree. Tired and hot, I hiked back to the car.

"This will cool you off." Mum turned on the air conditioning. "You think Bill is having fun?"

"He's having a great time," I said.

"Are you?"

"Wonderful. I like Sanibel."

And I was having a wonderful time. After a dinner of lobster and key-lime pie, we noticed children roller-skating near the restaurant. They wore hats of straw and waved sparklers. A boy in a Scout uniform passed one to

Bill, who lit it and spelled my name against the night. I watched the letters disappear, each before the fiery completion of the next.

Our bedroom was only an earlobe away from my parents', and this embarrassed us. We tried not to leave the living room at the same time, hoping staggered departures would conceal our eagerness. I stood, then Mum stood and invented a yawn, and we both said good night. Bill lingered with Robert and water polo highlights on television.

In our bathroom, I washed and approved my tan lines in the mirror. Then I started a mystery on top of the fresh sheets. I heard the announcer chanting penalties in the other room, Robert's and Bill's polite murmurs. I heard the waves, only inches outside the window. I wanted to throw a rock into the dark and hear how ominously close it would splash.

Bill came in. He slipped out of his cut-offs and pulled me down beside him on the bed. "All right," he whispered. "Let's play Scrabble." He folded my page corner. "Let's play Go."

We laughed and, as it turned out, didn't play anything. His skin was very sensitive. But I rubbed him with salve and he gripped my toes in his hand and named some after stars: Sirius the dog–toe, Nova-toe, and White Dwarf.

The day before leaving the island, we crossed the causeway at Punta Rassa and drove to Fort Myers. Robert wanted to exchange the Cougar, because its tires were dangerously bald. This done, we stopped for lunch and discussed doing something else on the mainland. I mentioned the swimsuit factory; Bill, the giant water slide. Robert announced we'd visit Edison's winter home.

Our guide was Naomi, from Land's End. She wasn't beautiful, but her English accent was charming. She said "spot of trouble," "bloody awful nights in the laboratory," and "a wee bit fou." Her skirt was polkadotted and above her knees, and she told the group she respected scientific methods. Bill smiled.

My parents confided in her immediately, saying "us three"—indicating themselves and me—were Canadian. They said we were in the Commonwealth together with her and shared the same queen. Naomi shook hands with them, but looked at Bill and asked where he was from.

"New York," he said. "The city."

We strolled through Edison's botanical gardens and learned about banyan trees, their roots dropping from the sky, tall bamboo, and goldenrod. Naomi showed us Mrs. Edison's walk, with flagstones donated by Ford and Firestone. We saw the swimming pool of Portland cement. We heard about Edison spitting on the floor, Edison sleeping standing up, Edison proposing to his second bride in Morse code.

Bill kept Naomi's pace and asked questions. She cited Edison's experiments to increase the life of the light bulb, his efforts at submarine detection. They seemed to be enjoying history.

I imagined them together. I was no longer slowly measuring my parents' steps and inspecting grounds. I saw Bill and Naomi in Cornwall: the cottage with a thatched roof; smoke circling the chimney; Naomi in a scanty apron, and nothing else, near the hob. They'd nurse Guinnesses and eat shepherd's pie together under quilts.

She would be a far better lover than I. The way she enunciated vowels and consonants, her choice of verbs, the way she moved her mouth were proof. She would call him different names at night, names he'd never heard before. She'd kneel and say, Beast, Master William.

Mum touched my shoulder. "Are you all right?"

"I'm fine."

"Why don't you go up there with Bill? You're missing the talk."

"I'm not missing anything."

Bill turned and waved, urging me closer to him and Naomi and the rest of the engrossed crowd. I shook my head and gestured towards my mother. "No," I mouthed.

By the time we entered Edison's laboratory, I hadn't pictured their children but had named them: Clarissa and Cyril and little Daphne. Even Robert had remarked upon the friendliness of the British. Bill and Naomi were at the front of the group, and when she stopped to comment on exhibits, Bill gave all his attention. I stared at him and willed another glance backwards to where I stood with my parents.

Finally I walked away. I said something to Robert—
"Sunstroke," maybe—and started running down the narrow aisle past Edison's sockets, fuses, and primitive
telegraphs. I passed a model of the Black Maria. I ran
by the glow of incandescent light and then was outside.

In the car on the way back, Bill marvelled at Edison.
The phonograph and the deaf man: how the subtleties of
music escaped him, but not sound. Mum argued that
Edison was brilliant and wondered which Canadian
could match him. Robert suggested Canada was known
more for humanitarians than for inventors. Then he
asked if we should buy ice for my head.

That evening my parents played marathon croquet on
a torchlit lawn.

"At last alone," Bill said.

We ate on the balcony, a supper of tossed greens, and
admired our sixth sunset. Bill perched on a pillow and
I leaned backwards against his chest. He twisted my
hair into two ponytails and tied them with strips that
usually secured celery.

"Sun sinks faster here," I said.

"Seems to."

"I always forget that the sun never sets." I turned to
look up at him. "That it's the earth turning away from
the sun."

He rested his chin on my head and placed his arms,
light as sleeves, over mine. "Still a *jolly good show* for
free."

Hours later we were still arguing.

"Where do you get these ideas?"

"You," I yelled.

"I asked you to move up."

"You didn't want me to."

"Next time I'll send a wire."

"Look," I said firmly, "you liked her."

"Smiling doesn't mean I want to lay somebody. I've told you this before."

"You're a liar," I said.

Bill grabbed my hair. I was pulled onto my feet and backwards into our bedroom. When he finally let go, I scrambled towards the closest wall and faced it. I was ashamed that the two of us—joyous wrestlers during sex—were now fighting to deliberately hurt. I thought of pets, confused by the familiar hand that feeds, strokes, then unexpectedly slaps.

"I don't know what to do, Adele." Bill sounded serious and sad. "I don't know how to make you believe me." I knew he was looking at me, waiting; then he went out.

I lay down on the bed and closed my eyes.

When my parents returned, after one, Bill was huddled on the balcony.

"Is he watching for satellites?"

"Doubt it," Robert said.

"Is he asleep?" I heard Mum open the sliding door. "Bill?"

"Maybe he's in the doghouse," Robert said.

They didn't say anything for seconds, and I guessed the exchange. My mother's referential eyes.

I suddenly heard Bill say hello, who won, too bad, good night. He came into our room without flipping on the lamp.

"Adele?"

I didn't answer.

"I think we should talk about giving notice when we get home. I don't know what's keeping us together anymore."

Next door, my parents undressed. I listened to the scrape of hangers in their closet and I heard them complain about their scores. I also heard our names, more than once.

We crossed Florida from west to east. The second and last reservation was at a Fort Lauderdale motel on North Atlantic Boulevard. Robert told us we were now off-season and rates were very reasonable.

The trip across Alligator Alley, Route 84, took five dull hours. Robert asked Bill if he cared to drive; he was delighted to, and Mum assumed his place in the back with me. Bill and I had barely spoken to each other over poached eggs, so it was doubtful we could have maintained enough back-seat small talk to amuse my parents, or fool them.

Mum talked about the tournament the night before,

how the hustlers had nudged their balls. "Nothing's sacred anymore," she said. "What did you two do last night?"

"Nothing, Mum."

"Took it easy?"

"Yeah. We ate supper and watched the sun go down." I looked out the window at a truck speeding in the other direction. It carried long palm trees, adults, on their sides. "You see that?"

"What?" Mum had missed it.

Bill braked needlessly and often. When a pelican swooped across the road, he applied his foot. When a car signalled left, station wagons away, Robert had to grip the dashboard. "Not used to power brakes," Bill said.

I noticed his strong hands on the wheel and remembered my scalp, how it had stung.

"So these are the Everglades!" Robert said.

The land was flat, the slash pines short and not exotic. It occurred to me we might be in a different hemisphere, that we'd ventured farther south than intended. Nobody lived there; no undershirts stiff on washlines; no dogs on porches, dead in sleep. Nothing to joke about or judge. But there were tourist attractions—six, three, one mile ahead.

"Want to go on an airboat?" Robert asked.

"Not really," I said. "Bill?"

He resisted looking at me in the rearview mirror. "Doesn't matter." He glanced at Robert. "But if you and June want to?"

"I'm not getting these feet wet," Mum said.

"Who knows when we'll be down here again." Robert folded a map of the Southeastern states. "Probably never."

I realized Bill and I were casting a pall over their trip.

The new suite, decorated in an avian motif, had only one bedroom, and my parents claimed it. Bill opened the couch in the combination kitchen, hallway, and living room. I found the linen, shook pillowcases spattered with parrots, and tucked in a blanket of faded blue wings and beaks.

"One more week," said Bill, not conversationally.

"That's right," I said. "Seven whole days."

Bill's younger brother, Donnie, worked summers at the Magic Kingdom in Orlando. Bill had written him from New York, listing dates and addresses, and he arrived before brunch on the third day of major gloom at Fort Lauderdale. Mum noticed his face and thought he'd been in a motorcycle accident.

"No," he said. "I stayed too long under the sunlamp." His skin was blistered and peeling; his swollen nose threatened his upper lip.

My parents loved him. He was familiar with Canadian sports and talked curling with Robert; he sliced crudités for Mum; he was fun. They invited Donnie to stay as long as he wished. And Bill and I were, if not congenial, more considerate of each other with the buffer of his company.

While Bill soaked in the bathtub, Donnie and I talked on a shaded patio and identified hookers pouting on the sidewalk. I picked out two.

"Three," Donnie said.

"Two."

"I'm not kidding, Adele."

"I'm not kidding either, kid. Look at her bag." I'd heard prostitutes favoured purses the size of chipmunks.

"She *is*."

"I'm not going to ask how you know." I loved Donnie, too. He was shorter than Bill, more muscular; he had a strong sense of right and wrong. He'd once knotted a cashmere sock around Bill's neck when he was suffering from a sore throat. He'd knocked out a college buddy who killed some dragonflies in the microwave for kicks.

I wanted to ask him about Bill. But Donnie was young; he still believed in the rewards of a suntan. I couldn't burden him.

Bill, in a motel towel, called from the door, and we tiptoed over hot concrete back to the room. Donnie bent to pluck the bottom leaf off a shrub.

"What's that?"

"Aloe." He straightened and showed me the lance-shaped shoot. "Juice is good for bites, rashes, burns—I'm going to use it on my face."

"You're an optimist." I hopped on one singed foot, then the other.

"Not really," he said. "Everything gets better eventually, anyway."

"That's optimistic," I said.

"Things can only get better. Right?" He held the aloe to his nose.

"Right."

"Some things get better faster if you just let them be." Donnie went on to describe the quick knitting of a kitten's broken leg, and how the vet had never been near it.

That night I encouraged Bill and Donnie to go out alone. "I'm going to stay here and write letters," I said. I also thought it would be a chance for them to talk and possibly review my virtues.

Bill kissed me on the top of my head. They said they wouldn't be late.

By three they weren't back, and I made a tarot spread of postcards on the coffee table. I asked the cards whether I should stoop to follow. A fisherman hugging a marlin, deep-sea charter boat boldly advertised behind him, pointed into my past; a lady water-skier, wearing a bikini the colour of bright persimmons, crowned me; a pale and bored flamingo anticipated my future; the final outcome was oranges. This card appeared twice. I couldn't fight the provocation of fruit. I borrowed Bill's kangeroo jacket and pulled up the hood.

The first bar I checked had held a wet nightgown contest earlier in the evening. The runners-up, in baby dolls and lace, still drank. The jukebox played Lesley Gore and they shouted the chorus, "It's my party and I'll cry if I want to." I ordered a Florida Key and, strangely, relaxed. I'd intended to be thorough: I was going to case every club, pizza nook, and parked car on the North Atlantic strip and catch them at seduction. But as I watched the other women swaying in flannels and satin, I recalled slumber parties where my girl friends had been accomplices in love: giving advice, keeping secrets. For a while, I forgot about Bill and the woman he was probably with.

A tractor driver from Gainesville introduced himself and offered me the world.

"Thank you anyway," I said.

On the way back, I passed unlit motels. I walked around a few courtyards and parking lots and counted room numbers. I wanted to pause and listen by each dark window, expecting to hear panting in a rhythm I would recognize. As if expecting to hear my own name in another's whisper.

When I unlocked the door in daylight, at our place, they were both dressed and asleep on the opened couch. Donnie wore one thin moccasin. I slipped it off, spilling sand on the blanket. I nudged Bill. He moved closer to the middle; I accepted his warm edge.

"There was a full moon last night." Donnie talked softly.

"I know."

"Bill and I got sick of bars and walked on the beach."

"How romantic," I said. "What time?"

"About three."

Donnie, Bill, and I were in bed. It was early morning and I'd brewed coffee to lure us into the day. Bill still slept between us.

"We were across from the Crab Shack when Bill spotted something on the tide." He sipped his coffee. "It was a turtle. Shell three feet wide."

"That's big."

He nodded. "She crawled onto the beach and started digging a hole with her back flippers."

"How'd you know she was a she?"

"Laying eggs," he said. "But we weren't sure. She could have been like those whales, you know—beaching themselves, dying—so Bill ran to the phone and called the SPCA."

"And they came?"

"Eventually. We'd already watched her lay the eggs and drag back to the ocean. She was incredibly weak." Donnie looked at Bill, his eyes slightly open even in sleep. "He called her Mama. *Come on, Mama*, he said. *You can make it, little Mama*. I thought he was going to pick her up and carry her."

I ran a finger along Bill's shoulder, over the slope and along the arm, until I reached his matching finger, its nail and top. I wanted to cry for that gentle side of him I'd missed.

"We showed the Turtle Patrol—they're the ones who came—where the eggs were buried, and they took them for incubation. They should be turtles in sixty days."

"With heat and luck."

"The guy said this one wouldn't hatch." He reached over and lifted an egg out of his other moccasin. I touched it. It was leathery, grey, heavier than a hen's.

"Where were you this morning?" Donnie asked.

"Turning tricks." I winked. "What else?"

"Bill was worried." Donnie took our mugs into the kitchen and refilled them.

I watched Bill sleep and wondered what would have happened if he and I had discovered the mother turtle in the moonlight. We might have talked about the mate she swam with only once, imagined conception off the Ivory Coast or Togo, offspring never to be seen. Witnessing this event might have made us kinder to each other.

We could have entered the Atlantic with her, then watched until she was our sorrow, out of sight beneath the waves.

Donnie headed back to Disney World that evening. He kept vigil in a haunted house, comforting terrified kids and pointing out "spirits" to the nearsighted, and had to go to work early the next day.

My parents stuffed French bread and Gouda into his rucksack and shook hands with him. Bill and Donnie embraced, then Donnie pivoted to face me; he lifted my chin with his forefinger. "Take care of the bro."

"I will."

"Don't think so much," he said.

He climbed onto his bike and raced the motor. He shouted thanks again; Robert said it was a pleasure, any time. Donnie turned to the north, his face glazed with aloe, one hand held steady in the air.

That night Bill and I slept together, by ourselves. We took turns rubbing: Bill asked for percussion and I steadily drummed with the sides of both hands up and down his spine. Then he scratched me, almost roughly, all over.

We were kissing when we heard my parents' door open and Robert squeezed by our bed. He turned on the stove light, six feet away from us, poured a glass of water, and sipped it. My vision was partly obscured by Bill's arm, but I caught the eerie gleam of Robert's white pajamas. I saw his tired face. He looked at the window and seemed to study his own reflection. Then he placed his glass in the sink, turned off the light, and groped the same way back. It was so quiet I couldn't hear our hearts. Bill and I waited in the new dark.

My mother and I got drunk in a bar named the Plucky Duck. She was buying; it was the last whole day of Florida; she'd quarrelled with Robert.

"Men," she said, over gin.

Robert and Bill had driven to Flagler Dogtrack to gamble on greyhounds. My stepfather, after research, anticipated returns on Silver Streak, Cat's Meow, or Bite. Bill, against all odds, was betting on Jupiter.

"A good fight clears the air." Mum tried to convince herself. "But so does a quick divorce."

They had disagreed about the maid. Mum said the

rooms didn't need tidying, since we were checking out soon. Robert said we were paying for the service, so they should be cleaned. If we were already paying, she said, why had he overtipped the nubile Cuban girl every single day? Robert replied he'd felt sorry for her and told Mum to drop the subject.

She now sat, swinging her legs, on a tall stool beside me. Young boys shot melodramatic pool behind us. One of them sank the eight on his break and swore.

"Do you know how to play?" she asked me.

"Nope."

"Does Bill?"

"He's good."

"I like Bill," she said. "Remember some of the fellows you used to go with? The one who used to sleep in his car in front of the house? What was his name?"

"I forget, Mum."

"Used to brush his teeth in the birdbath."

"He did not."

"He did. I saw him one morning."

"He never owned a toothbrush."

"He drove you to work every day until his car was repossessed." Mum pushed my hair behind my ear. "I think Bill cares for you very much."

"I think so." And with that I admitted, to myself, what I'd always known. I was Bill's only lover; I would continue to measure every other woman with his eyes: will she be the one? We had jogged on Riverside, in winter, and his eyes had loved a stranger's round ass and stride. I remembered snow and how cold the day had been. I remembered ice, pale as fingernails, arresting the Hudson.

Robert and Bill were cleaned out at the track, so Mum and I treated them to the movies. Mum chose the retrospective festival at Hialeah Drive-In: *An American in Paris* and *Gigi*. The cashier's hut displayed a historical plaque, and Robert held up the line to read it.

"This was once a grove," said Robert. "Ruby-red grapefruit. And then it was the biggest farmers' market in the Sunshine State. Did you know that, Beauty?"

Mum surveyed the paved lot. "Hard to believe anything ever grew here."

Robert parked behind the projectionist's booth. A Volvo pulled in, on our right, and the two schnauzers of an elderly couple barked at us and scrambled from front to back side window.

"Somebody shoot them," I said.

Nobody parked on our left.

"I don't think it's ever going to get dark tonight," Mum said. "I heard it hailed in Toronto today." She still felt the liquid afternoon.

"It's spring," Bill said.

The cartoon began, Robert turned up the volume, and we watched faint disasters against twilight—characters dropping from cliffs, freezing, drowning, reappearing and asking for more.

"Can you two see?" she asked. Mum was far away

from Robert; she practically sat on the arm of the door.

"We see fine." Bill's finger tightened on the belt loop of my short shorts, pulled me closer.

During the first feature, my mother fell asleep. So did the dogs.

Bill asked me to walk to the playground with him during intermission. We filed, hand in hand, past rows of cars and heard the speakers answering each other across the lot. There were no children under the huge screen. We climbed the monkey bars and Bill hung upside down, by his knees, until he heard the jingle of coins falling. Then we searched for his lost change by the reflected light.

The second feature started. Bill and I stretched out on the bare ground and looked up.

"Bill," I said, "I want to tell you something."

He slipped his arm under my shoulders and pressed his nose against my cheek.

I told him about Donnie squeezing juice from spikes of aloe, believing a plant could cure his burn. And how if it didn't, he had faith in time, the powers of his own skin. I told Bill what I thought I knew: Nothing would make me trust him. Nothing. Not nature, time, or love.

"So I'll love you always," he answered. "We'll be unhappy forever."

THE EDGER MAN

When I was twenty-nine years old, with two young children, I moved across the river to live in quiet, more affordable Brooklyn. I was twice intimate with failures that seemed, at the time, irredeemable. I had earned my master's in anthropology, somehow assuming I would live my life in a tent on the tip of someplace in Africa, but due to a variety of circumstance and choice, I was teaching ESL—English as a Second Language—to Arab and Japanese businessmen in midtown. And, not willingly, I was divorced, even though I understood it was for the best.

I spent a lot of time thinking about love. Sometimes about how I had failed to sustain, or perhaps inspire, it in my marriage. Sometimes about how humans are born into this world without the ongoing promise of it from parents, or persons unknown whom the future holds. About how, if they were not loved, would they learn?

Before our children were born, I had loved Bill, my husband, with a love like a Mack truck speeding, and when Graham and then Jane arrived, I discovered a love necessary and dense as air. I often could not believe the deep pleasure I felt watching their dumbest actions—Graham leaning like a tired old man on his left elbow and brushing his teeth; or hearing him root for the Mets and parroting lingo like choke, balk, strike, Strawberry; or how Jane sucked the butter out of my cob of corn.

We didn't belong there. I would have liked to move back west where I was born and start our lives all over again. I wanted my children to grow up in a place where they could play hide-and-seek in a yard until dark, and walk to school under the sway of tall green trees, rather than stepping around souls laying themselves down to die a bit more each day. But since I wanted my children to know, and be known by, their father, for better or for worse, to be loved, I stayed.

Where I was raised out by the Pacific, every other child's father worked at the sawmill. They were sawyers, boom men, or new on the green chain. Mine was an edger man. First up at a logging camp near Desolation Sound, where he sawed cedars centuries old. Then, after he was enchanted by my mother, June, music, and her three children, and wed them, he wound up in Vancouver at Pacific Pine. There he cut cants. Mum was forty, he was pushing fifty, and in next to no time, a year, I appeared. He was taken, often, for my grandfather.

Back in 1959, Sundays were still for family. We rented a boat at Lost Lagoon and rowed around the fountain in the rain, while Humphrey (Dad to me) recited a poem from his London boyhood:

> *It was midnight on the ocean*
> *Not a streetcar was in sight.*
> *The sun was shining brightly*
> *And it rained all day that night.*

I dangled my hand in the water, dwelling on that rhyme for the longest time. My mother mentioned that sitting in a damp boat on a wet lake, listening to nonsense, wasn't her idea of entertainment.

And we drove all the way to the United States to ride the Octopus and roller-skate outdoors, past the border town of Blaine, to Birch Bay, where fun was loud and colours so rude and bright they slammed my eyes. Mum begged Dad to join her for a cold beer on tap, since taverns were open Sundays serving throngs of pagan Canadians, and he squinted and said he imbibed only if someone died. Ray tuned his guitar under a totem pole. Irene and Joyce, seventeen and fifteen, marched the beach in their striped Bermuda shorts.

I followed. "Supposed to watch me."

"So we are," Joyce said, and they took off, kicking up mouthfuls of sand, then turned and walked backwards and waved interminably like the hillbillies.

"I see," Irene's small voice carried, "you."

I bent over and wiggled, but when I looked between my knees, they were upside down and disappearing.

On the way home, Ray and my sisters laughed so much the back seat seemed like a faraway, jolly country. Ray whispered dirty-book jokes ("Ever read *Russian Passion*? By Natasha Bitaballoff?") that made Mum look away out the open window and snicker.

I sat wedged between her and my father. She reached over my straw-hatted head, scratched his neck, and said, "Cat got your tongue, Humphrey?" and in his calm, logical tone he said he was trying to digest his dinner. She patted my bare leg, "Cold?" and her hand travelled back to hold the purse in her lap.

When I whined to climb into the back seat, Ray reminded everyone I hadn't got my rabies shot yet, which made the girls hoot. Inspired, I lied that I had, and then my father spoke up, "Enough back there. Unless you want to become pedestrians," and the car was one again, united by quiet. We even passed stiff dead deer without adding to the count.

There was another Sunday when Dad ended up taking only me. This was after the arguments between Mum and him had begun and she'd started taking the other three children to matinees and staying out for supper.

We went in the car. He didn't talk. I lay across the back seat of the Chev and stared at his bald head, and at the thatch of black hair inside his ear. He parked, and we got out and walked towards the bright lumber right on the river. The heady scent of wet cedar was in the wind. Dad pointed to a sign and said, "Pacific—?"

"Pine," I answered. Dad believed I'd inherited his brains and often found ways to prove this.

"This is where I work," he said. "Your father is first edger man."

We walked up a steep wooden staircase and stepped inside. The sawmill stretched like a very long shack, big and dark, without rooms. The windows were without glass. When I looked out, I saw the river in the rain, and it seemed as if the mill had come unmoored and that we were floating down and out to the salt chuck. Our four legs strode into light, out of step, and back into dark, past a picture of Smokey the Bear, his back to black trees and wild white fire.

He told me the forests of Europe were shrinking, and that their trees had stopped growing, cut short, scorched by war. Our trees were among the tallest on the planet, so tall their tops couldn't be seen. Widowmakers he called them. Heartwood, the inside of a tree, was dead. Sapwood, the outside, was alive. To cut a tree down, he kept the saw in the same place. The tree wasn't going anywhere. Sooner or later, it fell. He looked for points of crooks or whorls of knots. He made an undercut. He talked about knaps, knars, stumps, and spars, and about all sorts of saws—bull, hula, muley, whip, and chain.

I didn't understand any of this, but I listened. He always talked to me as if I knew exactly what he was going on about—how he'd found an ingenious way to repair the lawn mower, or the principle of a V-8 engine.

Sometimes he realized he was speaking over my head, and he looked down at me with serious regard and said, "Adele? Are you *still* a child?" as if I were taking an extraordinarily long time to mature.

The other end of the mill jutted over the river. It was wide open, without a wall, and below us booms of logs bobbed like long crocodiles. Dad put one hand on the railing and looked down. "Stinkwood," he said. "Hemlock."

I stood beside my father with my hand in his big one. Sometimes he let me bite tiny slivers of wood out of his hand. I felt a longing deep inside, but didn't know for what. I was light as sawdust in a palm, as if I could be blown away at any moment.

On the walk back, Dad stopped to explain his machine, the edger. He had taken his pen out and was drawing a diagram, and before I was even conscious of what I intended, I bolted away down the aisle, off balance in my rubber boots, and ducked down inside a booth. I waited, wild inside.

It took only a few seconds. "Adele." He was piqued. "Don't be an idiot. A sawmill is dangerous. It is not the place for a child to play."

I laughed.

I heard his slow, steady tread. He was close. I caught a glimpse of his red plaid shirt coming even with me, and then he stood still. We were both quiet for the longest time. Outside, a seagull cried like a cat. I stuck out my foot. "Warm," I whispered.

He was looking right at it, my foot, and then suddenly gazed directly over my head, past me, and quickly away, as if he hadn't even sensed me. He continued on, nonchalant. He kept going. "Dad?" I called out. He picked up his pace. "Dad?" I said again. "Cold, you're getting cold." I waited, and then didn't hear him anymore. I got up, shaking off flakes of sawdust. At the far end, he was turning to descend the stairs. He wasn't looking back. My heart hopped like a small bird in my chest. I wanted to be found. The whole point of hiding was to be found.

We left with just our clothes. The new house was empty, without an upstairs or curtains. If you opened a door in the kitchen, an ironing board fell and stuck out like a sick tongue. I was finally allowed a pet, a comatose turtle.

Mum saw quite a bit of Robert, who didn't stay with us but always seemed to be underfoot. Meals became more exciting because he was a little deaf and tremendously loud. He bought a movie camera at a police auction, and at the break of day, we burned under a blazing bar of light, eating breakfast, our names spelled in Alpha-bits on spoons. His hair was slicked back and shiny black. He always seemed to be kissing Mum or rubbing her feet, and he did that loudly, too. He called her Beauty.

I still didn't miss my father. I met children my age who all seemed to have drawbacks—crybaby, eczema, boring, pretty and always got picked to be princess. I often walked my turtle, wishing it were a dog. I spent most of my days exploring the field across the street, wild with clover and buttercups, full of garter snakes, puddles, prickles, and mad driven bees. I buried dead birds and made crosses of small white rocks. This was my hobby.

Nights, I knelt in front of the television set and changed channels for Ray, who said his wrist needed a rest. Or sometimes, after my bath, if it was a balmy, warm evening and nobody appeared at my bed to read a story, I wandered outside in my pajamas and watched Mum and Robert listen to a Mounties baseball game on the radio. They sat on the same side of the picnic table he'd built. He deciphered the plays for Mum, who seemed morally perturbed by runners stealing and wondered why they weren't pleased with the base they'd already reached. Sometimes Robert let on he knew I was there.

"Started counting the stars yet, Delbert?" Robert would say over his shoulder. "Because I'm going to ask you. I'm going to ask you how many there are."

"She can't count that high," Mum said protectively. "How high can you go?" Mum asked me.

"I'll check in the *Sun* tomorrow and see how many stars were out tonight. So you better start counting, Delbert."

"Don't call her Delbert, Robert."

"Wakey wakey, Delbert."

I would mumble a number, eight, or my favorite,

ninety-nine, and Mum gave a frilly laugh, Robert added something encouraging, and then they would forget I was there again. Some nights they listened to string music with sad singers, Judy Garland, Peggy Lee, and got all worked up about their divorces. By the end of summer, before I began grade one, the main topic was the detective hired to watch our house, and whose spouse was paying, or were my dad and Robert's wife in cahoots?

There were sudden new rules. Venetian blinds were kept drawn, even during a cloudy day, and Robert parked a block up the hill and rang the front doorbell before barging in whenever he wanted. Joyce was not allowed to linger necking in her boyfriend Eric's Zephyr; she had to drive away to hell and gone.

One night I woke up, looked out the window, and thought I saw him standing on the lawn just staring at me. I roused Ray.

He said, "You're cruising for a bruising," but finally got up and went back with me to the living room and pried open the blinds. His hand shook, then he made it shake more, and I laughed. "Nobody," he said. Then I had to get him a frosty Molson's. He gave me sips and let me watch part of a war epic with him, to calm down.

The next time I got scared, Ray wasn't home, and I crawled in with Mum without telling why. I didn't want to worry her. "Who's that?" she said perkily. "My Mince Pie?" Then I placed my frozen feet on her hot calves, and she said, "Go to sleep, Mince."

"I can't."

She pushed my pajama top up to my neck and played piano on my back, any song I wanted, "Away in a Manger," "Wonderful Wonderful Copenhagen," anything, and I heard it in her fingertips, in that soft force.

I didn't see my father until I was ten years old and he came to pick me up to go ice skating at Queen's Park rink. The divorce was final; he'd lost custody and been granted access every second Saturday. He was close to sixty. Mum shooed me out the door with a banana. She also handed me a dime: "For if there's a snit."

He waited in the green Chev, and wore the same outfit he was wearing the last time I remembered seeing him, Stanley Park Sunday clothes: a hat with a small red feather, herringbone jacket, blue tie with fish lures, solid blue shirt. He looked business as usual: slow, logical. He didn't seem mean, the goon who'd bled Mum by making her pay lawyers' holidays for years. He leaned over, opened the door, and said to keep the window down on my side; the muffler was on the blink and I could be poisoned by carbon monoxide. He meant to fix it someday. Once he'd turned onto Kingsway, he said, "Incidentally, do you recollect the rhyme?"

"No," I said.

"Oh." He looked away. "When you were young," he said, "you used to get frightfully upset and say, 'How could there be a streetcar on the ocean, Daddy?' You took it quite literally." He seemed saddened by my unreliable memory.

"Oh," I said. My legs were getting damp from the rain slicing in the open window, but I didn't shove over.

He inquired after "the Armstrongs"; I told him Joyce had eloped with Eric, and Irene married Peter—the Belgian boy from down the lane—and Ray was Casanova. I took it upon myself to inform him I was in grade five and got straight Bs.

At the rink, they played rock-and-roll. "Nigger music," Dad announced, then moved overly briskly into the thick of a pack of hunched boys. I hugged the side every few feet. The only way I knew to brake was to slam into the wood. The ice was strewn with teenagers, the normal sort and a mentally retarded bunch. One of them took over the penalty box, pounded his mitts together, and screamed "Santa" each time Dad whizzed by, until he was given a needle.

The light dimmed for the Couples Only, a ballad with lots of violin and philosophy. Dad stopped with a crisp *shmoosh*. Shaved ice skimmed off his blade. He stuck out a hand.

"But it's *couples*."

"We pass," he said, out of breath, "muster."

I took skittery steps to keep up, then let myself be towed. A rinkrat passed and said, "Who's holding up who?" Meanwhile, Dad said the only time he'd skied, he'd enjoyed it immensely, so much so he swore never to do it again. He mentioned Wormwood Scrubs in London, England, and about how if he didn't eat all his dinner, his psychotic mother sent him over to sit on the prison steps. The song seemed to go on for a complete century or two.

At Hudson's Bay on the way home, he bought me Barbie's "Tennis, Anyone?" outfit and a young-adult biography of Mary, Queen of Scots, which I started to read right away. We ate supper at the White Spot and dined in the car with a tray suspended parallel to our necks. He inevitably brought up Robert, whom he blamed for the breakup of the marriage and the loss of his family. He told me Wily Kiely wasn't the first boyfriend that the adultress had gotten chummy with. I didn't believe it. "My mother's not an adultress," I said. "She said she would have left you whether Robert moseyed along or not."

Dad kept chewing. He looked straight ahead. He said, "I don't believe that for one instant." He thought of Mum as a wayward child, without will or common sense, lured away.

"You weren't affectionate, she said."

He spoke perfunctorily: "That is simply not true." He took a sip of his tea. "Did you know that your mother, like my own mother, thought I was to blame for everything? If it was raining, she would attribute that to some malicious wish on my part."

When we ended up back at Mum's, I got out of the old

Chev, didn't answer his farewell, and, arms full of the day's loot, walked into the house and slammed the door. Nobody was home anyway.

I knew my mother hadn't loved him, not the way she'd loved Ray, Irene, and Joyce's dad. She still missed their father. She braided my hair into two tight twigs before school one morning and said she had dreamed again about the original Ray, Ray Senior. "I didn't want to wake up," she said. "It seemed so real. I just wanted to talk with him some more. God, he looked well."

"Did you ever love my dad?" I asked. I knew he still loved her in his way. He didn't date other old ladies; he lived like a hermit.

"I wanted to," she said. "I tried."

After one of my regular Saturday arguments with Humphrey, I pictured him driving home in his car—tired after the heavy meal and movies, discouraged after our row—and saw him falling asleep at the wheel. Switching lanes without signalling, which was his habit, and being in a car accident and dying, and all this without ever being loved. By his mother or mine. I went into the kitchen, picked up the phone, dialled, and heard it ring, over and over, my eye on the clock, and thought, *He should be home by now, this is enough time.* I started to pray. "Please let him be all right. Let him get home okay. Let him answer the phone," until I heard the click and his calm, annoyed voice say, "Hul-lo." I hung up.

.　　.　　.

Mum and Robert's honeymoon consisted of a two-week cruise to Anchorage: Mum was playing the Hammond organ during happy hours, and Robert was master of ceremonies and maracas. He kept time, those little beans stinging the beat. Mum had figured on taking me along, but Robert alarmed her with talk of icebergs.

I didn't want to stay at Dad's. His house was filthy. Mum and Irene had put up wallpaper after I was born—a pattern of hundreds of the same little Mexican boy feeding chickens—and his smiles and sombreros and hens were lost under thick dark soot. The hook for my Jolly Jumper still hung in the hall. He watched strictly CBC on an old boxy, black-and-white television in the kitchen, with his feet up on the coal hopper. After his retirement, he did odd jobs—mowing people's lawns, chopping and stacking wood.

When he inquired about the "wedding event," I didn't know what to say. I told him about Groucho, our Corgi, sprung from the basement of our new split-level home, slurping up drinks left by folding chairs outside on the patio. He'd gotten sloshed and I'd spent the next day by his basket, holding his paw through the hangover. I didn't tell him about Robert's tearful toast to the bride, which had a female guest writing his words down on a drink napkin; I didn't tell him how snug and right Mum and Robert looked dancing together. My father didn't ask any more about it.

Our last night together, we went to an opera. I'd never

been to one before, although he'd always wanted to take me. This was a big-city touring company, condescending to play their extravaganza in the provinces en route to Seattle and San Francisco. I wore what I'd worn to Mum's wedding. Dad dressed up. He'd shrunk in recent years, so his frayed trouser cuffs tickled the ground and the herringbone jacket seemed huge, but the shirt and light blue tie Mum had picked out for me to give him that Christmas fit fine. "All you need to know," Dad said, "is that everybody kicks the bucket and sings a horrendously long time while doing so."

It was *Tosca.* I didn't understand a word, but the music was shockingly beautiful. Towards the end of Act I, there was a scene at the font of the church. It built slowly, with organ, and the chorus kneeling, crossing themselves, singing the Latin Mass until they were in full voice, with cannons blasting, bells pealing wildly, and the heralding of trumpets. I was enraptured. Then I heard his noisy breathing. My father's shoulders shook and tears poured down his face and dripped onto his jacket.

I poked him in the side. "Dad," I said. "Your nose is running."

He didn't have a handkerchief, and I didn't have tissues, and he had to wipe his nose on his jacket sleeve. Somebody behind us passed along a starched white one, saying, "Keep it. You'll need it later." As Scarpia kneeled, almost humble, and confessed that his passion had made him forget God, Dad wiped his face. He shook his head in bewilderment at himself. "And not a soul has died," he said.

At the intermission, I told him if he was going to bawl like that, I would leave him and watch from standing room. He promised he wouldn't exhibit that behaviour again and he didn't. Everyone else cried, even I, and he sat there, his chin propped in his right hand, with bright dry eyes.

I completed grades eleven and twelve in one year, went back east, to U. of T., the University of Toronto, for a traumatic semester, then returned to British Columbia and majored in cultural anthropology. After my bachelor's, I forged ahead with graduate work and lived in the Arctic for a winter researching my thesis. A plane flew into the village once every two weeks with mail and supplies. Mum wrote with news of disasters and siblings, getting her hair done, and the new dog's bad breath. I didn't hear from my father.

I boarded in the little village of Igloolik, high above Hudson Bay, with an Inuit couple, Abel and Molly Pawlangtuk. They had lost their three children: by drowning, by exposure, by birth—strangled by the cord. They joked around and called me "Nanook," and "white daughter." I had my own room in their generic government house, sometimes ate meals with them—frozen caribou brought down from our roof, or tasty narwhal guts—and was free to come and go.

I was studying the effects of Christianity on the Inuit

belief in shamanism, so I spent a lot of time at Masses and evensong, and at teas with parishioners. I also attended faith-healing missions, watching locals faint, Pentecostals speak in tongues, and the blind point to the flickering flame of a candle, seeing the light for the first time. I asked a lot of questions about their conception of God. What did He look like? Describe Jesus. What did shamans do and where had they gone? Were there any shamans living in the village now?

I also, unethically, dated a shaman. Dated isn't the word; we were lovers. He was far older than me, although I never learned his true age, and his skin was soft and smoother than mine. When we came in from a walk on ice, he pulled off my high-tech mitts, lifted up his parka, and pressed my hands to his abdomen. He licked my lashes and ate the ice from my brows. He shot our food. He took good care of me. Since it was night a fair chunk of the day, we spent a lot of time in his bed under bearskins. My body had never been healthier, leaner, more exercised, more loved. Before we fell asleep, he said, "*Igluksak.*"

"Snow you can build with."

"*Aput.*"

"Snow just lying on the ground."

"*Piqtuq.*"

"Snow blowing in a blizzard."

"*Ganik.*"

"Falling snow."

"*Mauya.*"

"*Mauya* is soft, deep *sotto sotto* snow." I kissed him everywhere. "For lying down and making angels." I learned the meaning of *quviannikumuit*. To feel deeply happy. *Nuannarpoq*. To take extravagant pleasure in being alive.

Then one day I woke up feeling guilty about him and quickly ended it. He left the village soon after, and nobody knew where he'd gone. Many villagers thought he'd turned himself into a polar bear and flown away, but nobody publicly admitted to the old beliefs.

After the winter solstice, when the sun no longer appeared, I grew quite depressed. I didn't want to get out of bed and stayed under the caribou, listening on my recorder to tapes of the Talking Heads, *La Bohème*, or Dire Straits. I could not work. I walked with Molly through the village, down to the shore, where life seemed to be gradations of white and grey, and boats were packed off ice, and dogs were tied up, howling, below roofs holding carcasses of seal. I was living alone on a new planet. Abel said it was cabin fever. The government nurse prescribed an anti-depressant, which I didn't take, and handed me a stack of old *People*s. The Catholic priest visited, though aware I was an atheist, and held my hand while we read prayers aloud together. Then he suggested I go home for a breather. I wasn't sure where home was anymore.

Flying south took seven hours, two flights. I remember the jolt of joy when the treeline appeared, dark, a five o'clock stubble on the face of the blank earth. Timber.

Two years later, my father flew to New York for my sudden, small wedding. It was his first trip on a plane and he was terrified. In fact, he had not planned to attend the ceremony; he'd wanted to send my mother, as she and Robert were strapped. But Robert was in the hospital with a hernia and Mum wouldn't budge from his bedside. I prepped my fiancé. "Dad's a Brit Canuck. Jewish means Mottl the Tailor. He doesn't know we're expecting." In fact, nobody but us knew about the wee one. We were marrying so that Bill would be able to support us by securing lucrative scientific drudgery with the Canadian government up north.

At LaGuardia, my father was already deep in conversation with a shabbily dressed woman. Actually, he was similarly attired. People gave them looks. I embraced him—shorter, frail, afloat in his shirt—and, when he started to introduce us, tugged him aside. "Dad, that's a bag lady."

"Is that so?" he said, not registering. "She was relating an interesting tale about her involvement with your Jewish mayor."

A troupe of teen ballerinas giraffed by. "The bunheads are coming," the bag lady said. "Pay attention. Bunheads."

"And what exactly are the bunheads?" Dad asked as

a porter hustled us along. His balance was poor and he couldn't negotiate the multitude, but shook off my arm. I slowed and we caught up to his medieval suitcase at the curb.

Bill squealed up in the car. "Mr. Nordstrom," he said. "Mottl the physicist." My father warmed to him and started telling about the bag lady and Mayor Koch, whom he seemed to think Bill might know or be related to.

It was an intimate wedding—us. The justice of the peace informed my father he wouldn't be asking, "Who gives this woman?" and Dad said I'd not officially been his to donate to the fray for quite some time.

We dined at a semi-pompous Hicksville restaurant with valet parking. There were paintings of fox hunts and a zoo of overdressed drinkers on the terrace. It turned out they were another wedding soaking up the open bar. Our waiter told us it was the bride's second go-round at this venue. When she bore down upon the *chuppah*, Dad craned for a view. Her gown was fifties, long, low-cut. "A magnificent specimen," Dad said; then Bill stood up and ogled, too.

From there we drove to a motor inn in Elmhurst, Queens, the international crossroads of the world and close to both airports. Bill checked us in and ordered double wake-up calls. In the elevator, he shook my father's hand. "Thanks, Dad," he said, "for raising a specimen."

"Oh, you're welcome," Dad said. "Although I don't think I had much to do with it."

Bill got out and I helped my father to his room, floors above ours. "Did I hear correctly?" he said. "Did your rabbi call me Dad?"

"You heard," I said. I flopped in a chair. We were leaving the next day for low season in Negril, courtesy of Dad, and he was flying back to Vancouver. "You didn't have to come," I said.

"Oh, I wouldn't have missed it for the world." He eased himself down onto the bed.

"How's your jet lag?"

"Don't have it." He looked exhausted. "Let's see. It would be 9 p.m. back in Vancouver. Do you think perhaps you should call your mother? She might be worried."

I shook my head no. Outside, the traffic from Manhattan snarled by; someone with a horn played "La Cucaracha," which irritated me.

"That's 'La Cucaracha,' isn't it?" Dad said. In admiration, he added, "They do seem to have *everything* in the States."

I turned on the air conditioning and we listened to it. Here I was on my wedding night with my father, sitting on a bed, possibly a vibrating one, in a Queens motel.

"Marriage," Dad said, "as I'm sure you've learned during your extensive and, need I add, expensive schooling, is life's most difficult proposition."

"There are no happy marriages," I said. "Only unexamined ones."

"Who says that?"

"Me," I said.

The phone rang. Dad was delighted. "Now, who would be paging me *here*?" He answered it and looked confused for a second. "There's no Mrs. Stein," he said. "You've got the wrong number."

"Dad," I said. "That's me now."

Somewhat embarrassed, he passed the receiver, then bent to pore over the Spanish instructions for the vibrating bed.

"Room service?" It was Bill on the line. He'd obviously popped the champagne. "Hurry up. Send down a hot goy girl or I'm at the bar."

"Great," I said, ticked. "Go to hell." I hung up, breathed, smiled, and said to my father, "I'm going now."

"So soon?"

"Dad," I said, "it's my wedding night. I'm the bride. It's the big day. The big deal."

His hand gripped the headboard and he pulled himself up onto his feet. We trod over to the door. I smelled the woodsmoke caught in his jacket, the odour of home. A burglar had recently broken into his old house; Dad had been in bed, engrossed in a book on British Columbian shipwrecks, and hadn't heard the window below shatter. Nothing was taken. Nothing to take. The police figured it was a homeless person seeking a roof to sleep under, who thought the house abandoned.

We hugged long and couldn't quite let go of each other. He did not talk. Neither did I. It crossed my mind that I was holding my baby, his only grandchild, against him. But I did not speak up and tell him what was hidden inside. I let go of him. "So long," I said. "Time to fly."

"Oh," he said. "It is getting late."

"Yes," I said. "It is." I backed out. "Okay. Bye. Safe trip."

I pulled the metal door shut behind me. I heard him finally bolt it. Then, after three tries, it was gently chained.

MARINE LIFE

In July I visit my mother and we drive directly from the bus station to a car wash, even though her Dodge shines. She likes the slow tracks engaging the wheels, the car in neutral, the thought of hot carnauba wax. An attendant collapses the aerial and tells her to keep her foot off the brake.

"It's like driving under the ocean," Mum says. "I knew the fins on this old Dodge were meant for something."

Mops swathe the car in suds and giant bristles hum above us, then drag across the hood, roof, and sides. Her hands droop over the steering column and she stares straight ahead, although she can't possibly see through the lathered glass. "Come here once a day sometimes," she confides.

"Why so often?"

"It's kind of fun." She winks at me. "It's dark."

An overhead vacuum dries the car after the rinse. We watch the drops of water creep unnaturally up the slope of the windshield and disappear. She tells me this vacuum will often draw a migraine out through her temples, and I mention the trick my husband knows, how Bill can gently press the circle of his mouth to my forehead and take away pain. We laugh about that.

In daylight again, she turns the ignition and we start towards home. "I wish they lasted longer," she says.

We sit on the patio and watch the sprinkler waver back and forth, into sun, into shade. I grew up on this patio. I flooded it in winter and practiced for Rink Cadettes, skating into dizziness. We sip ginger ale while waiting for supper to cook.

"Remember when you used to run through the sprinkler in your birthday suit?"

"Yup."

"Remember when you used to run through the sprinkler in Robert's galoshes?"

That was before they could afford a wading pool. Now my mother and stepfather, rich on credit, discuss installing a real pool in their backyard, even though summers are brief and mythical in Vancouver. The grandchildren might enjoy it.

"How do you feel, Adele?" She means my pregnancy.

"With my hands." I look over, but she doesn't get it. "Fine. I just want pizza all the time."

"Thought of names?"

"Not yet."

I'm visiting my mother because she wants me to learn mothering. She wants her intuition and skill to rub off on me somehow, as softly and easily as scented oil. And I ask her about delivery—should I be localized, should I keep a piece of the umbilical cord, take a bite of the umbilical cord, should there be music?

"Every birth is different," she begins, happy in authority. "You'll know when the time comes."

Mum's spine is shrinking and tightens like a wet braid. Our heights don't match anymore—I lean over slightly to see the haphazard part in her hair. Earlier, when we husked corn in the kitchen, she asked, "Adele, did you feel the floor tilt?" And I said no, but the fault line *did* extend as far north as Canada and we were overdue. "I lose my balance once in a while," she admitted, ripping a green sleeve. "It's the planet moving, I'm sure."

She is sixty-five, my stepfather fifty-three, and this difference pinches her sleep, her face. Each night before bed, her hands slippery with cold lanolin, she coaxes suppleness back into her skin. "I keep busy," she says proudly.

We listen to the lawn mowers. They sound like a small war in the distance.

Mum introduces me to her ceramics instructor. "This is my daughter Adele, who's going to be a mother, too," speaking as if conception is our family's unique personal achievement.

She shows me what she has made: two white antelope for the mantelpiece, mugs with the family's names— June, Robert, my sisters Irene and Joyce, my brother Ray—and Bill's and mine still to be sanded; a flowerpot in the shape of a hippopotamus, glazed shakers wobbly on chicken legs, a stork for Q-tips.

"Mum, have you ever tried to shape anything on a potter's wheel? Or throw clay?"

"No."

"Maybe you should try."

"I paint everything myself," she stresses. "That damn hippo took three days."

A group of schoolchildren trot over to the kiln. They've made an octopus family, plaques for the bathroom, and they want to test the bubbles that will be suspended above them. I turn around and notice my mother bending happily with the seven-year-olds, checking.

After supper one night I ask if she will play the piano. Mum plays without sheet music, from memory, songs with notes that sit far off upon the ledger lines. I always ask myself how her brain knows where every finger should pause. How she carried on a conversation about where my mittens might be when her hands were reaching for something else, some black key.

When I was younger she played for fashion shows, nurses' graduations, cocktail hours, cabarets. She gave out a card with a golden treble clef: *June Will Be Pleased to Play Your Request*. She dressed thematically and wore muumuus and thongs for tropical shows, a chocolate suit for funerals, and a tiny rhinestone tiara on New Year's Eve.

She signed contracts with Tiki Tai, Town and Country, Coconut Grove, and the Elks' Club. I knew these were not the Hollywood clubs written up in magazines, but I believed they were the hotspots of the Lower Mainland, branches of a continental chain. It wasn't until I was older and could drive that I noticed these cabarets were out on the highways, parked on suburban edges. The Tiki Tai is now the O.K. Corral, the Town and Country topless, and the other two lost to fire.

After a certain age, I never knew aunts and uncles. I knew waitresses, chefs, managers, and sub drummers (my mother's steady drummer had recurrent heart attacks). She and Robert held dinner parties and invited staff, not other musicians or relatives. My brother, Ray, dated a coat-check girl my mother knew. She also introduced him to dancers in the Polynesian floor show, and it wasn't uncommon to see paper leis dangling from the knob of his closed door.

I went to drive-in movies with my stepfather while Mum played and played. We saw *The Manchurian Candidate*, *The L-Shaped Room*, and much of the *Flubber* series. We also played a word game on our way to pick her up, using the billboards and neon signs as the clues. Robert would say, for instance, What's a frisky pig? And I would scan the print in sight for the next two blocks and find Buckingham Cigarettes illuminated in bold letters above me and shout. Since we always drove the same route, the game eventually became predictable and we listened to call-in talk shows on the radio instead. The announcer said, "Hi, doll," to the women callers and listened to them complain about Gerda Munsinger, German spy, sleeping with Cabinet ministers. Robert started calling my mother Doll.

In 1965 her contract at the Simon Fraser Dining Room was not renewed. This gig was elegant, downtown, and Mum wept on her piano bench at home. An Oriental woman, Sue Kim or Kim Lu, had been hired and she was classical. Twenty-two.

"Let me be the man in the family," Robert said. "You don't have to work anymore."

"They think I'm old," she said.

He made phone calls to the Musicians' Union and a rival dining room. Ray and I drove to the grocery in his convertible and bought smokes and doughnuts. He told me she cried for Robert's attention.

When we returned, Mum was practicing scales—majors, minors, chromatics—sliding up and down ivory, and she did this the whole afternoon.

Tonight she says, "You might have heard these before," and plays music to inspire labour: "I Can't Give

You Anything But Love, Baby," "Yes Sir, That's My Baby," "Baby Face." She still has that touch.

"You're a tourist now," Mum declares, even though I was born and raised here. "You live up north."

"I don't live 'up north.' I live only one day away."

"Osoyoos is up north," she says, and decides to show off Vancouver. She won't let me drive, claims I'm not used to automatic, and I won't fit behind the steering wheel anyway.

We stop at the Planetarium and she selects a postcard for Bill, now working at the sky-watch site in Manitoba. She's found the Crab Nebula, a magnified photograph of space. "Send this to your stargazer," she suggests. We both write messages, each picking up the other's last word and carrying it a few phrases further.

"Why don't we go up the mountain and look at the view, Mum?" I say. "There's no fog."

She chooses the scenic route and we skirt the ocean— the nudists at my old haunt, Wreck Beach, and families at Locarno and Jericho. When we reach the north shore she can't locate the exact turn and makes lefts, a few rights, guessing randomly, even follows the sign with an arrow pointing straight up. "I thought I could drive here in my sleep," she says. "Are we even climbing uphill?"

"Yes." And we are. The car has geared down, the air is crisper, and I glimpse the snow on Grouse above us, but she is still lost. She won't accept my help.

My mother opts for a tall hill, closer to home and accessible. The view is less spectacular than broad, and she claims she can distinguish the Gulf Islands twenty miles distant. I can't see that far.

One evening Robert thumbs through my prenatal manual and finds it pretty funny. He puts mats on the grass and we try exercises together—Mum, him, and me—sprawling on our backs and hugging knees close to our foreheads. We inhale in unison and relax by isolating different areas of the body—wrists, thighs, shoulders—tightening and releasing. This exercise takes ten minutes done thoroughly and Robert ends up drowsing with his mouth open.

Mum and I go into the house and she hands me two needles caught in a fistful of soft wool. "He's knitting a bootie for you," she explains.

"For me?"

"For the baboo. And I'm doing its twin."

I can't believe it, can't picture his longshoring hands clicking needles. "Since when does he knit?"

"Since lately," she says. "Sometimes he's not tired when I conk out, so he decided there's not much difference between counting stitches or sheep." She adds, "I chose the pattern."

I get upstairs to bed before they do and hear them evaluating a new Toyota while doing dishes. Robert wipes and estimates their trade-in worth. Folding my hands on my stomach, I speak slowly to my baby. "Where you had little buds, you have arms and legs, my little tidal wave. And now you have eyelashes, and now you have toenails." I'm certain it can hear, only three months from birth, and my mother says it's sensitive to light; she's read babies can tell night and day before they see it.

I hear Mum turning on the news and then I worry about my tactless nerves carrying sensations, uncensored, to the amniotic fluid: a sadness while stroking my mother's roses; the shock when the phone rings because I hope it's Bill and that he's all right. I wonder what my baby might already know.

Mum wakes me. "It's a bad dream." Her hand shakes my shoulder. "Adele, it's all right."

I sit up and look at her, groggy and nightgowned, on the edge of the bed. I'm in my old room, unfamiliar without my trappings: a collection of starfish, books on shamanism; totem poles. It's the spare room now, bare except for ivy cuttings. "I'm not having a bad dream."

"I heard you," she says. "You were yelling in your sleep."

"Damn it, Mum. You woke me up." I settle back down.

"*You* woke me."

"It was probably a train whistle."

"It was you."

I'm certain it wasn't. I vaguely recall dreaming about Bill and me driving through Wyoming and think she's woken me on purpose.

"Come have a cup of tea," she offers. "You'll feel better."

We hobble downstairs in our slippers and prepare tea and cinnamon toast. She remembers when I used to fight with people in my sleep. How she and Robert would be turning off the lights, or tucking our dog into his basket with a biscuit, and I'd scream, "Shut up," or "Go to hell, you dumb cluck," and make Groucho bark.

"Who were you so mad at?"

I don't know. I'm tired and want to go back to bed, but she's awake and ready to chat—about Ray's common-law love, about a brunch she's booked to play for Job's Daughters, how she must rehearse.

About 2 a.m. she fetches a small china box and places it before me. She opens it and spreads tiny molars and bicuspids and incisors on the table, beside our saucers, and tells me it's my first set of teeth.

"You're kidding," I say.

"No," she whispers. "I'll always keep your teeth."

The next morning Mum asks if I'll go to her swimming class. It's held at the same complex as her ceramics workshop. The recreation centre runs several programs for seniors and she takes square dancing as well. "Do-si-do," she calls to me, coming out of the bathroom, and back to back, we switch places.

Tomorrow I catch the bus to my home in the Interior. I realize I haven't called my sister Irene yet, Ray, my hermit father, and have spent all my time with her and Robert. I say, "Yes, I'll come to your lesson."

When my mother stopped playing seriously, I was in junior high school. Only time on my hands, she said, and volunteered for the Christmas concert, embarrassing me with the amount of hair spray she used. She appeared for the oil refinery field trip, an unwanted chaperone, and pouted when I didn't sit with her. "Someday you'll wish you could ride on a bus with your mother," she said to me as she squeezed by. Once, she offered to pick me up after school and go for a shake. I saw her car approaching and ducked behind a hedge, and waved her airily on when she slowed, anxious.

She shopped and brought home blouses with big perky bows or hats that would sell big in Antarctica, furry things I refused to wear, socks with toes, and then apologized. "I know my taste is all in my mouth," she said. Even last birthday, when she mailed Snoopy sheets, she wrote, "If you and Bill want to return them, I have the receipt."

She packs for her swimming class: a fluffy towel, hairdryer, shampoo and conditioner, bathing cap, a suit with her Floaters crest prominent on the abdomen, and unnecessary goggles. She hasn't yet learned how to put her head under water and keep her eyes open.

At the pool she entered the changing room with other older ladies. "Hello, June," they say. "Hot today." They enjoy this ritual of totebags and lockers and a teacher telling them what to do.

I watch Mum change. Her stomach is loose and her legs are scarred from vein stripping, thigh to heel. She struggles with her suit and I clasp it for her at the back.

"Adele, why don't you take a dip?"

The other ladies seem to agree it would be refreshing. "Don't exert yourself, though, honey." Mum asks the instructor about my shorts and tank top and she says they'll be okay. The water will be soothing.

The class won't pay attention at first. They bob up and down in the pool, comparing gardens and bantering about the odd-even sprinkling rules. Mum playfully flicks water in my direction.

The instructor has them do widths using a paddle-board. My mother kicks with the rest of them, slowly, and crosses the pool. Then they practice their frog kick. These older women, uneasy amphibians, are more of land than water. They roll in the small current they create, and some surrender to the swell and kick solely from the knee, forgetting the glide. Their bones are brittle. Break a leg when you're sixty and it may never mend. And so a few just turn over on their back and float.

They are supposed to learn the basics of the modified breaststroke today. Mum has mentioned it—how difficult it will be to coordinate arms, legs, and lungs. "As you glide, your chin lifts," the instructor explains, "and you inhale. Then, as you stroke, exhale."

I see my mother crossing the pool, going away from me; her breathing is erratic and rapid. The paddleboard supports her chest, but only her legs lend motion, as her arms reach out awkwardly. I'm nervous now: I realize we are all in the same water. I sense my baby drifting inside, and look at my mother, flailing towards the other side, and I am in between, some kind of lifeguard in the shallows.

WHITE SHOULDERS

My oldest sister's name is Irene de Haan and she has never hurt anybody. She lives with cancer, in remission, and she has stayed married to the same undemonstrative Belgian Canadian, a brake specialist, going on thirty years. In the family's crumbling domestic empire, Irene and Peter's union has been, quietly, and despite tragedy, what our mother calls the lone success.

Back in the late summer of 1984, before Irene was admitted into hospital for removal of her left breast, I flew home from New York to Vancouver to be with her. We hadn't seen each other for four years, and since I didn't start teaching ESL night classes until mid-September, I was free, at loose ends, unlike the rest of her family. Over the past months, Peter had used up vacation and personal days shuttling her to numerous tests, but finally had to get back to work. He still had a mortgage. Their only child, Jill, who'd just turned seventeen, was entering her last year of high school. Until junior high, she'd been one of those unnaturally well-rounded kids—taking classes in the high dive, water ballet, drawing, and drama, and boy-hunting in the mall on Saturdays with a posse of dizzy friends. Then, Irene said, overnight she became unathletic, withdrawn, and bookish: an academic drone. At any rate, for Jill and Peter's sake, Irene didn't intend to allow her illness to interfere with their life. She wanted everything to proceed as normally as possible. As who wouldn't.

In a way, and this will sound callous, the timing had worked out. Earlier that summer, my ex-husband had been offered a temporary teaching position across the country, and after a long dinner at our old Szechuan dive, I'd agreed to temporarily revise our custody arrangement. With his newfound bounty, Bill would rent a California town house for nine months and royally support the kids. "Dine and Disney," he'd said.

I'd blessed this, but then missed them. I found myself dead asleep in the middle of the day in Jane's lower bunk, or tuning in late afternoons to my six-year-old son's, and Bill's, obsession, *People's Court*. My arms ached when I saw other women holding sticky hands, pulling frenzied children along behind them in the August dog days. So I flew west. To be a mother again, I'd jokingly told Irene over the phone. To serve that very need.

·   ·   ·

Peter was late meeting me at the airport. We gave each other a minimal hug, and then he shouldered my bags and walked ahead out into the rain. The Datsun was double-parked, hazards flashing, with a homemade sign taped on the rear window that said STUD. DRIVER. "Jill," he said, loading the trunk. "Irene's been teaching her so she can pick up the groceries. Help out for a change." I got in, he turned on easy-listening, and we headed north towards the grey mountains.

Irene had been in love with him since I was a child; he'd been orphaned in Belgium during World War II, which moved both Irene and our mother. He'd also reminded us of Emile, the Frenchman in *South Pacific*, because he was greying, autocratic, and seemed misunderstood. But the European charm had gradually worn thin; over the years, I'd been startled by Peter's racism and petty tyranny. I'd often wished that the young Irene had been fondled off her two feet by a breadwinner more tender, more local. Nobody else in the family agreed and Mum had even hinted that I'd become bitter since the demise of my own marriage.

"So how is she?" I finally asked Peter.

"She's got a cold," he said, "worrying herself sick. And other than that, it's hard to say." His tone was markedly guarded. He said prospects were poor; the lump was large and she had the fast-growing, speedy sort of cancer. "But she thinks the Paki quack will get it when he cuts," he said.

I sat with that. "And how's Jill?"

"Grouchy," he said. "Bitchy." This gave me pause, and it seemed to have the same effect on him.

We pulled into the garage of the brick house they'd lived in since Jill's birth, and he waved me on while he handled the luggage. The house seemed smaller now, tucked under tall Douglas firs and fringed with baskets of acutely pink geraniums and baby's breath. The back door was open, so I walked in; the master bedroom door was ajar, but I knocked first. She wasn't there. Jill called, "Aunt Adele?" and I headed back down the hall to the guestroom, and stuck my head in.

A wan version of my sister rested on a water bed in the dark. When I plunked down I made a tiny wave. Irene almost smiled. She was thin as a fine chain; in my embrace, her flesh barely did the favour of keeping her bones company. Her blondish hair was quite short, and she looked ordinary, like a middle-aged matron who probably worked at a bank and kept a no-fail punch recipe filed away. I had to hold her, barely, close again. Behind us, the closet was full of her conservative garments—flannel, floral—and I understood that this was her room now. She slept here alone. She didn't frolic with Peter anymore, have sex.

"Don't cling," Irene said slowly, but with her old warmth. "Don't get melodramatic. I'm not dying. It's just a cold."

"Aunt Adele," Jill said.

I turned around; I'd forgotten my niece was even there, and she was sitting right on the bed, wedged against a bolster. We kissed hello with loud smooch effects—our ritual—and while she kept a hand on Irene's shoulder, she stuttered answers to my questions about school and her summer. Irene kept an eye on a mute TV—the U.S. Open—although she didn't have much interest in tennis; I sensed, really, that she didn't have any extra energy available for banter. This was conservation, not rudeness.

Jill looked different. In fact, the change in her appearance and demeanour exceeded the ordinary drama of puberty; she seemed to be another girl—shy, unsure, and unable to look me in the eye. She wore silver wire glasses, no makeup, jeans with an oversize kelly-green sweatshirt, and many extra pounds. Her soft straw-coloured hair was pulled back with a swan barrette, the swan's eye downcast. When she passed Irene a glass of water and a pill, Irene managed a swallow, then passed it back, and Jill drank, too. To me, it seemed she took great care, twisting the glass in her hand, to sip from the very spot her mother's lips had touched.

Peter came in, sat down on Jill's side of the bed, and stretched both arms around to raise the back of his shirt. He bared red, hairless skin, and said, "Scratch."

"But I'm watching tennis," Jill said softly.

"But you're my daughter," he said. "And I have an itch."

Peter looked at Irene and she gave Jill a sharp nudge. "Do your poor dad," she said. "You don't even have to get up."

"But aren't I watching something?" Jill said. She glanced around, searching for an ally.

"*Vrouw*," Peter spoke up. "This girl, she doesn't do anything except mope, eat, mope, eat."

Jill's shoulders sagged slightly, as if all air had suddenly abandoned her body, and then she slowly got up. "I'll see you after, Aunt Adele," she whispered, and I said, "Yes, sure," and then she walked out.

Irene looked dismally at Peter; he made a perverse sort of face—skewing his lips south. Then she reached over and started to scratch his bare back. It was an effort. "Be patient with her, Peter," she said. "She's worried about the surgery."

"She's worried you won't be around to wait on her," Peter said, then instructed, "Go a little higher." Irene's fingers crept obediently up. "Tell Adele what Jill said."

Irene shook her head. "I don't remember."

Peter turned to me. "When Irene told her about the cancer, she said, 'Don't die on me, Mum, or I'll kill you.' And she said this so serious. Can you imagine?" Peter laughed uninhibitedly, and then Irene joined in, too, although her quiet accompaniment was forced. There wasn't any recollected pleasure in her eyes at all; rather, it seemed as if she didn't want Peter to laugh alone, to appear as odd as he did. "Don't die or I'll kill you," Peter said.

Irene had always been private about her marriage. If there were disagreements with Peter, and there had been—I'd once dropped in unannounced and witnessed a string of Christmas lights whip against the fireplace and shatter—they were never rebroadcast to the rest of the family; if she was ever discouraged or lonely, she didn't confide in anyone, unless she kept a journal or spoke to her own God. She had never said a word against the man.

The night before Irene's surgery, after many earnest wishes and ugly flowers had been delivered, she asked me to stay late with her at Lion's Gate Hospital. The room had emptied. Peter had absconded with Jill—and she'd gone reluctantly, asking to stay until I left—and our mother, who'd been so nervous and sad that an intern had fed her Valium from his pocket. "Why is this happening to her?" Mum said to him. "To my only happy child."

Irene, leashed to an IV, raised herself to the edge of the bed and looked out at the parking lot and that kind Pacific twilight. "That Jill," Irene said. She allowed her head to fall, arms crossed in front of her. "She should lift a finger for her father."

"Well," I said, watching my step, aware she needed peace, "Peter's not exactly the most easygoing."

"No," she said weakly.

We sat for a long time, Irene in her white gown, me beside her in my orange-and-avocado track suit, until I began to think I'd been too tough on Peter and had distressed her. Then she spoke. "Sometimes I wish I'd learned more Dutch," she said neutrally. "When I met

Peter, we married not speaking the same language, really. And that made a difference."

She didn't expect a comment—she raised her head and stared out the half-open window—but I was too shocked to respond anyway. I'd never heard her remotely suggest that her and Peter's marriage had been less than a living storybook. "You don't like him, do you?" she said. "You don't care for his Belgian manner."

I didn't answer; it didn't need to be said aloud. I turned away. "I'm probably not the woman who can best judge these things," I said.

Out in the hall, a female patient talked on the phone. Irene and I both listened. "I left it in the top drawer," she said wearily. "No. The *bedroom*." There was a pause. "The desk in the hall, try that." Another pause. "Then ask Susan where she put it, because I'm tired of this and I need it." I turned as she hung the phone up and saw her check to see if money had tumbled back. The hospital was quiet again. Irene did not move, but she was shaking; I found it difficult to watch this and reached out and took her hand.

"What is it?" I said. "Irene."

She told me she was scared. Not for herself, but for Peter. That when she had first explained to him about the cancer, he hadn't spoken to her for three weeks. Or touched her. Or kissed her. He'd slept in the guestroom, until she'd offered to move there. And he'd been after Jill to butter his toast, change the sheets, iron his pants. Irene had speculated about this, she said, until she'd realized he was acting this way because of what had happened to him when he was little. In Belgium. Bruges, the war. He had only confided in her once. He'd said all the women he'd ever loved had left him. His mother killed, his sister. "And now me," Irene said. "The big C which leads to the big D. If I move on, I leave two children. And I've told Jill they have to stick together."

I got off the bed. "But, Irene," I said, "she's not on earth to please her father. Who can be unreasonable. In my opinion."

By this time, a medical team was touring the room. The junior member paused by Irene and said, "Give me your vein."

"In a minute," she said to him, "please," and he left. There were dark areas, the colour of new bruises, under her eyes. "I want you to promise me something."

"Yes."

"If I die," she said, "and I'm not going to, but if I do, I don't want Jill to live with you in New York. Because that's what she wants to do. I want her to stay with Peter. Even if she runs to you, send her back."

"I can't promise that," I said. "Because you're not going to go anywhere."

She looked at me. Pale, fragile. She was my oldest sister, who'd always been zealous about the silver lining in that cloud; and now it seemed she might be dying, in her forties—too soon—and she needed to believe I could relieve her of this burden. So I nodded, *Yes*.

.   .   .

When I got back, by cab, to Irene and Peter's that night, the house was dark. I groped up the back steps, ascending through a hovering scent of honeysuckle, stepped inside, and turned on the kitchen light. The TV was going—some ultra-loud camera commercial—in the living room. Nobody was watching. "Jill?" I said. "Peter?"

I wandered down the long hall, snapping on switches: Irene's sickroom, the upstairs bathroom, the master bedroom, Peter's domain. I did a double-take; he was there. Naked, lying on top of the bed, his still hand holding his penis—as if to keep it warm and safe—the head shining. The blades of the ceiling fan cut in slow circles above him. His eyes were vague and didn't turn my way; he was staring up. "Oh, sorry," I whispered, "God, sorry," and flicked the light off again.

I headed back to the living room and sat, for a few seconds. When I'd collected myself, I went to find Jill. She wasn't in her downstairs room, which seemed typically adolescent in its decor—Boy George poster, socks multiplying in a corner—until I spotted a quote from Rilke, in careful purple handwriting, taped to her long mirror: "Beauty is only the first touch of terror we can still bear."

I finally spotted the light under the basement bathroom door.

"Jill," I said. "It's me."

"I'm in the bathroom," she said.

"I know," I said. "I want to talk."

She unlocked the door and let me in. She looked tense and peculiar; it looked as if she'd just thrown water on her face. She was still dressed in her clothes from the hospital—and from the day before, the kelly-green sweat job—and she'd obviously been sitting on the edge of the tub, writing. There was a Papermate, a pad of yellow legal paper. The top sheet was covered with verses of tiny backward-slanting words. There was also last night's pot of Kraft Dinner on the sink.

"You're all locked in," I said.

She didn't comment, and when the silence stretched on too long I said, "Homework?" and pointed to the legal pad.

"No," she said. Then she gave me a look and said, "Poem."

"Oh," I said, and I *was* surprised. "Do you ever show them? Or it?"

"No," she said. "They're not very good." She sat back down on the tub. "But maybe I'd show you, Aunt Adele."

"Good," I said. "Not that I'm a judge." I told her Irene was tucked in and that she was in a better, more positive frame of mind. More like herself. This seemed to relax Jill so much, I marched the lie a step further. "Once your mum is out of the woods," I said, "your father may lighten up."

"That day will never come," she said.

"Never say never," I said. I gave her a hug—she was

so much bigger than my daughter, but I embraced her the same way I had Jane since she was born: a hand and a held kiss on the top of the head.

She hugged me back. "Maybe I'll come live with you, Auntie A."

"Maybe," I said, mindful of Irene's wishes. "You and everybody," and saw the disappointment on her streaked face. So I added, "Everything will be all right. Wait and see. She'll be all right."

And Irene was. They claimed they'd got it, and ten days later she came home, earlier than expected. When Peter, Jill, and I were gathered around her in the sickroom, Irene started cracking jokes about her future prosthetic fitting. "How about the Dolly Parton, hon?" she said to Peter. "Then I'd be a handful."

I was surprised to see Peter envelop her in his arm; I hadn't ever seen him offer an affectionate gesture. He told her he didn't care what size boob she bought, because breasts were for the hungry babies—not so much for the husband. "I have these," he said. "These are mine. These big white shoulders." And he rested his head against her shoulder and looked placidly at Jill; he was heavy, but Irene used her other arm to bolster herself, hold him up, and she closed her eyes in what seemed to be joy. Jill came and sat by me.

Irene took it easy the next few days; I stuck by, as did Jill, when she ventured in after school. I was shocked that there weren't more calls, or cards, or visitors except for Mum, and I realized my sister's life was actually very narrow, or extremely focused: family came first. Even Jill didn't seem to have any friends at all; the phone never rang for her.

Then Irene suddenly started to push herself—she prepared a complicated deep-fried Belgian dish; in the afternoon, she sat with Jill, in the Datsun, while Jill practiced parallel parking in front of the house and lobbied for a mother-daughter trip to lovely downtown Brooklyn for Christmas. And then, after a long nap and little dinner, Irene insisted on attending the open house at Jill's school.

We were sitting listening to the band rehearse, a *Flashdance* medley, when I became aware of Irene's body heat—she was on my right—and asked if she might not want to head home. She was burning up. "Let me get through this," she said. Then Jill, on my other side, suddenly said in a small tight voice, "Mum." She was staring at her mother's blouse, where a bright stitch of scarlet had shown up. Irene had bled through her dressing. Irene looked down. "Oh," she said. "Peter."

On the tear to the hospital, Peter said he'd sue Irene's stupid "Paki bugger" doctor. He also said he should take his stupid wife to court for loss of sex. He should get a divorce for no-nookie. For supporting a one-tit wonder. And on and on.

Irene wasn't in any shape to respond; I doubt she would have anyway.

Beside me in the back seat, Jill turned to stare out the window; she was white, sitting on her hands.

I found my voice. "I don't think we need to hear this right now, Peter," I said.

"Oh, Adele," Irene said warningly. Disappointed.

He pulled over, smoothly, into a bus zone. Some of the people waiting for the bus weren't pleased. Peter turned and faced me, his finger punctuating. "This is my wife, my daughter, my Datsun." He paused. "I can say what the hell I want. And you're welcome to walk." He reached over and opened my door.

The two women at the bus shelter hurried away, correctly sensing an incident.

"I'm going with Aunt—" Jill was barely audible.

"No," said Irene. "You stay here."

I sat there, paralyzed. I wanted to get out, but didn't want to leave Irene and Jill alone with him; Irene was very ill, Jill seemed defenseless. "Look," I said to Peter, "forget I said anything. Let's just get Irene there, okay?"

He pulled the door shut, then turned front, checked me in the rearview one last time—cold, intimidating—and headed off again. Jill was crying silently. The insides of her glasses were smeared; I shifted over beside her and she linked her arm through mine tight, tight. Up front, Irene did not move.

They said it was an infection which had spread to the chest wall, requiring antibiotics and hospital admission. They were also going to perform more tests.

Peter took off with Jill, saying that they both had to get up in the morning.

Before I left Irene, she spoke to me privately, in a curtained cubicle in Emergency, and asked if I could stay at our mother's for the last few days of my visit; Irene didn't want to hurt me, but she thought it would be better, for all concerned, if I cleared out.

And then she went on; her fever was high, but she was lucid and fighting hard to stay that way. Could I keep quiet about this to our mother? And stop gushing about the East to Jill, going on about the Statue of Liberty and the view of the water from the window in the crown? And worry a little more about my own lost children and less about her daughter? And try to be more understanding of her husband, who sometimes wasn't able to exercise control over his emotions? Irene said Peter needed more love, more time; more of her, God willing. After that, she couldn't speak. And, frankly, neither could I.

I gave in to everything she asked. Jill and Peter dropped in together during the evening to see her; I visited Irene, with Mum, during the day when Peter was at work. Our conversations were banal and strained— they didn't seem to do either of us much good. After I left her one afternoon, I didn't know where I was going and ended up at my father's grave. I just sat there, on top of it, on the lap of the stone.

The day before my New York flight, I borrowed my mother's car to pick up a prescription for her at the mall.

I was window-shopping my way back to the parking lot, when I saw somebody resembling my niece sitting on a bench outside a sporting goods store. At first, the girl seemed too dishevelled, too dirty-looking, actually, to be Jill, but as I approached, it became clear it was her. She wasn't doing anything. She sat there, draped in her mother's London Fog raincoat, her hands resting on her thickish thighs, clicking a barrette open, closed, open, closed. It was ten in the morning; she should have been at school. In English. For a moment, it crossed my mind that she might be on drugs: this was a relief; it would explain everything. But I didn't think she was. I was going to go over and simply say, *Yo, Jill, let's do tea*, and then I remembered my sister's frightening talk with me at the hospital and thought, *Fuck it. Butt out, Adele*, and walked the long way round. I turned my back.

One sultry Saturday morning, in late September— after I'd been back in Brooklyn for a few weeks—I was up on the roof preparing the first lessons for classes, when the super brought a handful of mail up. He'd been delivering it personally to tenants since the box had been ripped out of the entrance wall. It was the usual stuff and a thin white business envelope from Canada. From Jill. I opened it: *Dearlingest* (sic) *Aunt Adele, These are my only copies. Love, your only niece, Jill. P.S. I'm going to get a job and come see you at Easter.*

There were two. The poems were carefully written, each neat on their single page, with the script leaning left, as if blown by a stiff breeze. "Black Milk" was about three deaths: before her beloved husband leaves for war, a nursing mother shares a bottle of old wine with him, saved from their wedding day, and unknowingly poisons her child and then herself. Dying, she rocks her dying child in her arms, but her last conscious thought is for her husband at the front. Jill had misspelled wedding; she'd put *weeding*.

"Belgium" described a young girl ice skating across a frozen lake—Jill had been to Belgium with her parents two times—fleeing an unnamed pursuer. During each quick, desperate glide, the ice melts beneath her until, at the end, she is underwater: "In the deep cold / Face to face / Look, he comes now / My Father / My Maker." The girl wakes up; it was a bad dream. And then her earthly father appears in her bed and, "He makes night / Come again / All night," by covering her eyes with his large, heavy hand.

I read these, and read them again, and I wept. I looked out, past the steeples and the tar roofs, where I thought I saw the heat rising, toward the green of Prospect Park, and held the poems on my lap, flat under my two hands. I didn't know what to do; I didn't know what to do right away; I thought I should wait until I knew clearly what to say and whom to say it to.

.   .   .

In late October, Mum phoned, crying, and said that Irene's cancer had not been caught by the mastectomy. Stray cells had been detected in other areas of her body. Chemotherapy was advised. Irene had switched doctors; she was seeing a naturopath. She was paying big money for an American miracle gum, among other things.

Mum also said that Jill had disappeared for thirty-two hours. Irene claimed that Jill had been upset because of a grade—a C in Phys Ed. Mum didn't believe it was really that; she thought Irene's condition was disturbing Jill, but hadn't said that to Irene.

She didn't volunteer any information about the other member of Irene's family and I did not ask.

In November, Bill came east for a visit and brought the children, as scheduled; he also brought a woman named Cheryl Oak. The day before Thanksgiving, the two of them were invited to a dinner party, and I took Graham and Jane, taller and both painfully shy with me, to Central Park. It was a crisp, windy night. We watched the gi-normous balloons being blown up for the Macy's parade and bought roasted chestnuts, not to eat, but to warm the palms of our hands. I walked them back to their hotel and delivered them to the quiet, intelligent person who would probably become their stepmother, and be good to them, as she'd obviously been for Bill. Later, back in Brooklyn, I was still awake—wondering how another woman had succeeded with my husband

and, now, my own little ones—when Irene phoned at 3 a.m. She told me Jill was dead. "There's been an accident," she said.

A few days later, my mother and stepfather picked me up at the Vancouver airport on a warm, cloudy morning. On the way to the funeral, they tried to tell me, between them—between breakdowns—what had happened. She had died of hypothermia; the impact of hitting the water had most likely rendered her unconscious. She probably hadn't been aware of drowning, but she'd done that, too. She'd driven the Datsun to Stanley Park—she'd told Irene she was going to the library—left the key in the ignition, walked not quite to the middle of the bridge, and hoisted herself over the railing. There was one eye-witness: a guy who worked in a video store. He'd kept saying, "It was like a movie. I saw this little dumpling girl just throw herself off."

The chapel was half-empty, and the director mumbled that that was unusual when a teenager passed on. Irene had not known, and neither had Mum, where to reach Joyce, our middle sister, who was missing as usual; Ray, our older brother, gave a short eulogy. He stated that he didn't believe in any God, but Irene did, and he was glad for that this day. He also guessed that when any child takes her own life, the whole family must wonder why, and probably do that forever. The face of my sister was not to be borne. Then we all sang "The Water Is Wide," which Jill had once performed in an elementary-school talent show. She'd won Honourable Mention.

After the congregation dispersed, Peter remained on his knees, his head in his hands, while Irene approached the casket. Jill wore a pale pink dress and her other glasses, and her hair was pinned back, as usual, with a barrette—this time, a dove. Irene bent and kissed her on the mouth, on the forehead, then tugged at Jill's lace collar, adjusting it just so. It was the eternal mother's gesture, that finishing touch, before your daughter sails out the door on her big date.

I drank to excess at the reception; we all did, and needed to. Irene and I did not exchange a word; we just held each other for a long minute. From a distance, and that distance was necessary, I heard Peter talking about Belgium and memories of his childhood. On his fifth birthday, his sister, Kristin, had sent him a pencil from Paris, a new one, unsharpened, and he had used it until the lead was gone and it was so short he could barely hold it between his fingers. On the morning his mother was shot, in cold blood, he'd been dressing in the dark. The last thing she had said, to the Germans, was, "Don't hurt my little boy." This was when Mum and I saw Irene go to him and take his hand. She led him down the hall to his bedroom and closed the door behind them. "Thank God," Mum said. "Thank God, they have each other. Thank God, she has him."

And for that moment, I forgot about the despair that had prompted Jill to do what she did, and my own responsibility and silence, because I was alive and full of needs, sickness, and dreams myself. I thought, *No, I* will never tell my sister what I suspect, because life is short and very hard, and I thought, *Yes, a bad marriage is better than none,* and I thought, *Adele, let the sun go down on your anger, because it will not bring her back,* and I turned to my mother. "Yes," I said. "Thank God."